HIDDEN BLESSINGS

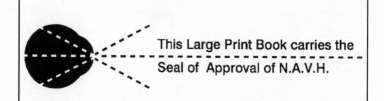

This Large Print Book carries the
Seal of Approval of N.A.V.H.

HIDDEN BLESSINGS

JANE MCBRIDE CHOATE

THORNDIKE PRESS

An imprint of Thomson Gale, a part of The Thomson Corporation

THOMSON

GALE

Detroit • New York • San Francisco • New Haven, Conn. • Waterville, Maine • London

LIBRARY OF CONGRESS CATALOGING-IN-PUBLICATION DATA

Choate, Jane McBride.
    Hidden blessings / by Jane McBride Choate.
      p. cm. — (Thorndike Press large print candlelight)
    ISBN 0-7862-9172-9 (alk. paper)
    1. Women clergy — Fiction. 2. Pet theft — Fiction. 3. Teenage boys — Fiction. 4. Large type books. I. Title.
PS3553.H575H53 2006
813'.54—dc22
                                                2006029085

U.S. Hardcover:
ISBN 13: 978-0-7862-9172-4
ISBN 10: 0-7862-9172-9

Published in 2006 by arrangement with Jane McBride Choate.

Printed in the United States of America on permanent paper
10 9 8 7 6 5 4 3 2 1

To Arianne Raquel,
our own sweet angel.

CHAPTER ONE

"Reverend Stevens . . . I mean, Reverend Hastings . . ." Thelma Harvey stopped, looking flustered, and twisted a lace-edged handkerchief in her hands.

Carla dropped the papers in her hand — Sunday's sermon — and ushered Thelma to the only comfortable chair in her office.

"What's wrong?"

"It's Grover Cleveland. He's missing. He's been gone for two days."

Carla bit back a smile. Grover Cleveland ran away at least once a week — usually on the weekends. He always returned by Sunday night, hungry and repentant.

"I wouldn't worry," she said gently. "Grover Cleveland will show up in time for his dinner on Sunday. Probably right after services."

"He didn't run away," the older woman said, continuing to twist the now crumpled handkerchief. "He's been stolen."

Carla thought about the sermon she had yet to finish, the basketball game she was due to coach in another hour, and dinner — alone — with Sam. She held back a sigh.

"What makes you think he was stolen?"

Thelma drew herself up. "It's obvious, isn't it? Grover Cleveland is a purebred."

Carla barely refrained from chuckling. If Grover Cleveland was pure anything, it was mutt. He resembled something between a beagle and a collie with a bit of poodle mixed in. "Why don't we wait and see if he shows up tomorrow?"

"And when he doesn't?" Thelma stood. "I must say, Reverend, that marriage doesn't seem to have improved your compassion for the helpless animals of the world. I admit that when I've come to you in the past about Grover Cleveland being missing, he's turned up the next day. But my baby's really gone this time. And you don't care. Nobody cares." She sniffed.

Carla pressed the older woman's hands in her own. "I'm sorry. Would it help if I searched the neighborhood with you?"

A watery smile touched Thelma's lips. "Would you? I'd feel so much better if I knew someone else was looking for him too. My grandson, Martin, is visiting. He would've helped me look, but he had some business to take care of. He's first in his medical school class, you know."

"I think you mentioned it once or twice," Carla said. In truth, Thelma had mentioned her grandson a great deal more than that.

"Martin's so good to come and visit me. But he won't be here forever. That's why I have to find Grover Cleveland." She dabbed at her eyes with her handkerchief. "He's all I have."

The hitch in her voice tore at Carla's heart. Her sermon could wait. She'd call Sam, ask him to substitute at the girls' game, and explain that dinner might be a little late. Again.

"But why does it have to be you?" Sam asked.

"I know Grover Cleveland," Carla said, pulling off her dress and changing into jeans and a sweatshirt. "Someone else might scare him off. Besides, Thelma needs me. I couldn't say no."

Sam sighed. He looked at his wife of six months and was reminded of why he loved her so much. "What kind of name is Grover Cleveland for a dog anyway?"

"Thelma's the great-great-grandniece of President Grover Cleveland. Or something like that. The current Grover Cleveland comes from a long line of Grover Cleve-lands. Dogs, that is. Not presidents."

A smile slipped past his annoyance. "Doesn't she ever call him Grover? Or Cleve?"

Carla pretended to look shocked. "Certainly not. He's named for a president of the United States. You don't shorten the name of a president. Even a dead one."

"Sorry."

"So you'll substitute at the game for me? I wouldn't ask, but Thelma is really upset. If you'd seen her — heard her — when she said Grover Cleveland is all she has . . . I couldn't let her look for him alone."

Any more than she could turn away the dozens of other requests that filled her life, Sam reflected. When Carla loved, it was with her whole self. He, more than most, had reason to appreciate that fact.

"I'll substitute for you on one condition."

She paused as she tied her sneakers. "What's that?"

"You promise to take the phone off the hook tonight and let me make dinner for the two of us."

"But if we take the phone off the hook, no one can —"

"Exactly."

Her lips curved into a smile. "You drive a

hard bargain, Councilman Hastings."

"I learned from the best, Reverend Hastings. Is it a deal?"

She reached up to kiss him. "Deal." She kissed him again, a slow, deep kiss that made him want to gather her to him and shut out the rest of the world. Before he could suggest it, she was waving goodbye. "I'll see you later."

Sam stared after her, exasperated, bemused, and totally bewitched. Marriage to Carla was more than he'd ever dreamed. It was also exhausting, he admitted two hours later, as he ducked to miss a ball. As an architect, his reflexes weren't often tested.

He wasn't fast enough.

"Sorry, Mr. Hastings," a girl said as they discussed strategy during halftime. "I didn't mean to hit you. Next time try to duck, okay?"

"It was my fault. I shouldn't have kept my eyes open."

The girls all giggled.

"You're not very good at basketball," another girl said. "But you're kind of cute. For an old guy."

"Thanks."

Whoever said that coaching a girls' basketball team was easy obviously didn't know what they were talking about, he thought, gingerly touching his left eye and trying to keep his right eye focused on the game. He raced up and down the court, trying to keep up with six teenage girls, all of whom exuded an energy he couldn't hope to match. Obviously he was more out of shape than he'd realized.

An accidental kick to his shin by a member of the opposing team made him clutch his leg while he squinted through his uninjured eye. He smiled around a grimace of pain and reminded himself that the game was nearly over.

When Sissie Marker scored another two points, bringing the final score to seventy-two versus sixty-eight, the girls screamed, rallying around her. Sam found himself as excited as anyone, cheering wildly and imagining Carla's reaction to the victory. She'd whoop as wildly as the girls.

"Anyone for pizza?" he offered.

The girls jumped on him, shrieking their delight. He worked his way out of the jumble of arms and legs and gasped for breath.

Sissie slapped him on the back. "You're all right, Mr. Hastings."

"Thanks. I think."

After a trip to the pizza parlor, where the team made numerous toasts with mugs of root beer, Sam limped home and consoled himself with the thought of a quiet dinner alone with Carla.

A dinner he still had to cook. A wry smile twisted his lips as he remembered his first attempt at cooking dinner for the two of them — charred steaks, underdone baked potatoes, and a limp salad.

Whistling softly, he started to boil a pot of water. Twenty minutes later, he deftly drained a pot of pasta.

When he heard the front door open, he set the pot aside and headed to the living room to see Carla.

Her face was smudged with dirt, her eyes shadowed with fatigue. For a moment Sam was tempted to give way to his anger. She gave too much of herself. She gave as she did everything — without half measures, without thinking of the cost to herself. It was the one source of contention in their marriage. Attempts on his part to persuade her to occasionally say no met with a serene smile and an unyielding stubbornness.

He did the only thing he could. He kissed her.

When she raised her head, she gave a low whistle. "You're going to have a beaut of a shiner tomorrow."

He grinned. "I'll just tell everyone it's my

wife's fault."

"My fault?"

He lifted a shoulder. "Sure. You're the reason I was coaching the team."

"Nice logic. Is that how you win arguments on the city council?"

"No. That's how I plan to get you to pamper me for the rest of the evening."

She stood on tiptoe and pressed a kiss to his lips. "How's that?"

"Not bad. Once more and I'll definitely be on the mend."

Smiling at his foolishness, she repeated the kiss. It lengthened, deepened, until she was clinging to him.

When he released her, Sam said, "I think we may have discovered a new cure for black eyes."

"I think maybe you're right." She sank onto the sofa, where she tried — unsuccessfully — to hide a yawn. She saw Sam's quick frown and managed a faint smile.

"Let me help you with your shoes." He tugged off her shoes and rubbed her feet.

"Mmm." She sighed her appreciation. "That feels so good. I think we must've covered every square inch of the neighborhood."

"Did you find Grover Cleveland?"

A frown chased away her smile. "No. We

14

searched the whole neighborhood. No one's seen him. Not even the Millers."

"The Millers?"

"Mrs. Miller has a toy poodle named Collette that Grover Cleveland courts on the weekends."

His lips twitched as he tried to hide a grin. "Courts?"

"You know, courts as in . . ." To Sam's delight, she blushed.

The grin got away from him just then, earning him a reproving look. "Yeah, I know. I just didn't know if Grover Cleveland did."

"Grover Cleveland is the neighborhood Lothario."

George barked.

"Except for George," she said, patting the head of their own favorite canine.

Sam chuckled. "Maybe Grover's hiding out. Afraid to come home and face the music." The smile he'd hoped to elicit didn't appear. "Hey, you're not really worried about old Grover, are you? He'll turn up. Didn't you say he does this every week?"

"I can't help it. This feels different. If something happened to him, I don't know what Thelma would do. She dotes on that dog."

"She could get another one."

"She loves Grover Cleveland, Sam. He's not just a dog to her. He's family."

He heard the soft reproach in Carla's voice. "I'm sorry. I didn't mean it the way it sounded."

"I know." She bent down to scratch George behind the ears. "How would you feel if something happened to George and someone suggested we just replace him?"

Sam looked down at the dog that had made himself one of the family some months ago. They hadn't chosen George; he'd chosen them. Sam never thought he'd admit it, but he'd miss the floppy-eared dog. "I get your point."

She brushed his cheek with the back of her hand. "I just wish I could have helped her."

"You did. You listened to her and tried to find him. That's a lot more than most people would have done."

"But it wasn't enough."

He took her in his arms, smoothing his hands down her back. "You can't fix everything that goes wrong in the world, Carla. No one can."

"You're right. I just wish . . ."

"I know. You want to make everything right." It was another one of the things he loved about her, her ability to put herself in the place of others. Too frequently, though, she was unable to draw the line between empathy and sympathy.

He felt her nod against his chest. "If Grover Cleveland doesn't show up by tomorrow, I'll help you look for him. Until then, we've got the whole evening to ourselves." He grabbed her hand. "C'mon. I fixed linguine with crab."

"You're a lifesaver."

"I know."

"Not to mention modest."

He bowed with a flourish.

An hour later, Carla pushed back her chair and sighed with unmistakable satisfaction. "For a man who couldn't even boil water when we were married, you've come a long way."

Sam smiled, her words bringing a warm flush of pleasure to his face. She hadn't been exaggerating. His cooking skills had consisted of heating up a microwave dinner and not much else. Although he doubted he'd ever be *cordon bleu* quality, he now cooked passably well. Just another one of the changes she'd wrought in his life.

She started to clear the table, but he stilled her hand. "You're beat. I'll take care of it."

She shook her head. "Uh-uh. We made a

deal. One person cooks and the other cleans up."

"In that case, why don't we do it together?"

They splashed in the sudsy water like two children. Wiping a bubble from her nose, he remembered the first time he'd helped her wash dishes. Then he'd only wanted to get to know the pretty woman minister better. Falling in love with her had never been part of his plan. But Carla had him doing a lot of things he'd never thought he'd be doing. Things like coaching a girls' basketball team. Things like cooking dinner and liking it. Things like . . .

She brushed her lips over his, wiping away rational thought — and every other kind.

He wound the dish towel around her waist, drawing her to him. "What did I ever do without you?"

"I don't know. But I'm not giving you a chance to find out."

That was all right with him, Sam thought, once more losing himself in the sweetness of her lips. More than all right.

Sam spent the following morning crawling beneath the underbrush surrounding Thelma Harvey's house, looking for Grover Cleveland. He turned up a boot, a pair of jeans, and an assortment of bones. But no dog.

He returned home tired, dirty, and looking for sympathy. George greeted him at the door, barking wildly.

"What's up with George?" he asked, brushing off clumps of dirt and leaves.

Carla appeared, holding a scruffy yellow rug to her chest. Sam stared in fascination as the rug wriggled in her arms and then jumped to the floor. Malevolent eyes stared up at him.

Instinctively he took a step back. "What's that?"

"His name is Thomas. He's a cat."

Sam held on to his exasperation with admirable calm. "I know *what* it is. What I don't know is what it's doing here."

"Not it. He."

"What is *he* doing here?"

"Thomas needed a home."

"Not another one," Sam muttered, but his voice held no anger, only resignation. And tenderness.

"Another what?"

"Another one of your strays."

"Thomas isn't a stray. I got him at the animal shelter."

"The animal shelter?"

"I went there with Thelma, looking for

19

Grover Cleveland. We thought someone might have found him and taken him there. He wasn't at the shelter, but I saw Thomas. The man there told me they were going to have to put him" — she lowered her voice — "to sleep. Because he'd been there so long and no one wanted him."

Sam looked at the shaggy yellow-haired creature and could believe it. The cat had to weigh at least thirty pounds. One ear was torn, the top half missing. His eyes weren't green, they were yellow. A venomous yellow, Sam decided.

Thomas jumped from Carla's arms to the chair to the table.

Sam swatted him with the newspaper. "Get down, you mangy beast."

Carla grabbed the newspaper away from Sam. "He's testing us. Seeing where the limits are."

Sam was very much afraid he was going to fail the test, but he had no chance to say so as Carla patted his arm.

"I'll admit he's a little lacking in the social graces, but he'll learn. He's very intelligent. You can see it in his eyes."

Sam looked at the yellow eyes and saw cunning. The cat had obviously conned Carla into believing he was sweet and docile, but Sam wasn't deceived. He tried again to remove the cat from the table, but Thomas merely glared at him.

"Carla, he's a tomcat. He belongs outside. Probably in an alley."

"That's where he was picked up. The man at the shelter thinks he was abandoned. Can you believe anyone would throw out a poor, defenseless animal to fend for himself?" She picked up the animal and cuddled him to her.

Thomas purred.

Sam eyed the big cat and decided he was a match for anything. Or anyone. His last owner had probably abandoned him in an act of self-preservation.

But he couldn't tell Carla that. She was already stroking Thomas' back, crooning to him and, unless Sam was very much mistaken, preparing to make him a permanent part of the family. He didn't delude himself that Thomas' stay would be only temporary. He'd been through this before.

He made a last-ditch attempt. "Don't you think he'd be happier on a farm or something? Someplace where he could catch mice?" Or rats, he added silently.

"Do you know anyone who owns a farm?" Carla asked reasonably.

"No."

She gave him a triumphant smile. "Then

21

we have to keep him. Besides, he'll be good company."

Sam took another look at Thomas, who was staring at him with undeniable challenge. "Good company for who?"

"Whom," she corrected absently. "George. You know how lonely he gets when we're both out. Now he won't sit and mope anymore. It's not good for him." She said it with such genuine pleasure that Sam couldn't argue with her. He tried logic instead.

"Carla, Thomas is a cat. George is a dog. Does that suggest anything to you?"

"They're both animals?"

He rolled his eyes. His gaze happened to connect with the cat's yellow-eyed stare. "How did he get Thomas for a name?"

Carla looked uncomfortable for the first time. "I named him on the way home from the pound. It seemed to fit."

He barely suppressed a groan. "Thomas the tomcat."

"Something like that." She began to rummage through the cabinets. "Now I just need to find something to feed him." Standing on tiptoe, she pulled out a can. "Do you think he likes salmon? Or tuna?"

Thomas meowed.

George barked.

Carla smiled.

Sam sighed. It looked like they owned a cat.

To Sam's annoyance, George and Thomas took to each other like long-lost friends. After sniffing Thomas thoroughly, George lay down on his belly, his paws stretched out in front of him. Thomas settled himself between George's huge paws, gave a decidedly feline yawn, and immediately went to sleep.

"I don't believe it," Sam muttered. "By all rights those two ought to be at each other's necks. Instead they're cozying up to each other like bosom buddies."

"They recognize each other as kindred souls," Carla said.

"Kindred what?"

"Souls. You know, they were both abandoned and now they've found a home."

"Our home," Sam added under his breath.

She smiled.

Her smile had the usual effect on him. "I'm going to the store," he said.

She looked up from where she was making a bed for Thomas by the stove. "What for?"

"Cat food."

Thomas made himself at home with an ease that set Sam's teeth on edge. It wasn't that Sam didn't like cats, he defended himself. It was just that Thomas didn't behave like a normal cat. Certainly Thomas didn't regard himself as common. He made that clear in the way he spurned ordinary cat food with icy disdain, demanding instead chopped liver, chicken, and tuna. Sam blamed Carla for that. Giving Thomas tuna the first day had established a precedent. An expensive precedent.

"It's either him or me," Sam declared wrathfully three days later.

Carla gave him what she hoped was a sympathetic look. "What's Thomas done now?"

Ever since they'd brought him home from the animal shelter, Thomas had staged an unrelenting war against Sam. Small incidents, such as stealing a favorite pair of his argyle socks, had escalated into guerrilla attacks that now verged on all-out warfare, with Thomas emerging as the undeniable victor.

Sam rolled his eyes dramatically. "That four-legged beast scarfed down the crab salad I made for our lunch. I went out of the kitchen for a minute — a minute, mind you — and, when I came back, he'd eaten the whole thing. Pasta and all."

Carla did her best not to laugh. "Maybe

he was hungry."

"Hungry? The fiend had just finished polishing off a can and a half of tuna. But is he satisfied with that? No. He wants our salad as well."

"We'll make some more salad," she said. "It won't take long."

"That was the last of the crab. Carla, I think you're missing the point. Thomas is a sneak thief. What's more, he's a thief who likes gourmet food. He'll be demanding steak pretty soon, with Champagne to wash it down with. It's bad enough he's drunk more often than not. Now he's a thief as well."

"He's not always drunk. It's not his fault he got a little tipsy on the cooking sherry. I was the one who left it on the counter."

"And Thomas just happened to knock it over and lick it up," Sam finished. He looked so indignant that she was hard put not to laugh.

"Thomas likes the good things in life. It probably comes from the deprived life he had to endure before he came here."

"Depraved is more like it," Sam said under his breath.

This time she couldn't stifle the laugh that erupted.

He glared at her. "Go ahead. Laugh all

you want. Just remember what I said. That cat is going to eat us out of house and home before we know it."

"I'll talk with him. Make him see the error of his ways."

"A lot of good that will do," Sam grumbled. "He knows he's got you twisted around his little paw." A smile played on his lips, and she knew he wasn't as furious as he pretended to be.

"I've got an idea. How about we go out for lunch? Just the two of us?" She grinned at him. "We won't even invite Thomas and George."

"Promise?"

"Promise. We'll go someplace quiet, someplace —"

The phone shrilled.

"Where the phone doesn't ring?" Sam asked, making a face as he picked up the receiver.

Carla listened as he made soothing noises into the phone.

"Give us a few minutes and we'll be there, Mrs. Miller." He turned back to Carla, his expression grim. "Collette's missing."

"That makes two."

"Yeah."

"She was right here on the porch," Mrs. Miller said, gesturing for Carla and Sam to have a seat several minutes later. "We were getting ready to take our walk, and I went back inside to get my gloves. She wouldn't have gone without me." She cast a baleful glance at the neighbor's house. "If I didn't know better, I'd think that Grover Cleveland was behind this."

"Grover Cleveland's missing too," Carla pointed out.

"I know that. Thelma Harvey was over here just yesterday and accused my Collette of luring away that mutt of hers. As if Collette would even be interested in a dog with such a stupid name." Mrs. Miller bristled, her ample bosom heaving. "The nerve of that woman."

Sam's shoulders shook, causing Carla to throw him a warning glance.

"Not that I don't love Thelma, you understand," Mrs. Miller went on. "She and I go back nearly thirty years. It's just that she's positively silly over that dog of hers."

Sam started to laugh and barely covered it with a cough just as Mrs. Miller looked up.

"Something funny, Sam?" she asked.

Carla frowned at him.

Caught, he started to stammer. "Uh . . . no. I was just thinking about where Collette could have gone."

Giving him a sharp look, Carla took the

older woman's hand and squeezed it. "We'll help you look for Collette. We'll find her, won't we, Sam?"

He nodded, wishing he believed she were right.

They spent the rest of the afternoon searching for Collette and came up with nothing. No one had seen anything. No one had heard anything. Collette had vanished, just as Grover Cleveland had.

Sam left Carla with Mrs. Miller and headed home. He sat on the kitchen stoop, trying to sort out in his mind what was happening. A gut instinct that he'd learned not to ignore told him something more was going on than just a couple of lost dogs.

Two dogs missing in less than a week. He ticked off the things they had in common. Both were mutts, valuable only to their owners. Both were well-known in the neighborhood. Of course, it could be a coincidence, but he didn't believe it.

If he didn't know better, he'd suspect the dogs had been kidnapped. But there had been no demands for ransom. Besides, Collette and Grover Cleveland belonged to elderly people of modest means. Any way he looked at it, it didn't add up.

Absently he scratched George behind the ears. If anything happened to George Carla would be devastated. Sam shook his head at the thought. Come to think of it, he'd feel pretty bad himself. George was a member of the family.

Sam hugged the dog tightly until George barked in protest. "Sorry, boy," Sam murmured. "I was thinking about something else."

George looked up with a soulful expression and gave a plaintive woof. He trotted to the kitchen door.

"Okay, I guess one extra dog biscuit wouldn't hurt."

The dog bounded inside the kitchen and Sam followed. Thomas entwined himself between Sam's legs, nearly causing him to trip.

Sam glared down at the cat. "You're a menace."

Thomas returned the glare with his unblinking gaze.

Carla returned home a short time later.

"Still no Collette?" Sam asked.

"I kept praying she'd just wandered off and would show up any moment, but . . ." She shook her head. "First Grover Cleveland and now Collette. When's it going to stop?"

Their gazes strayed to George.

CHAPTER TWO

The phone rang shrilly, and Carla rushed to answer it, but Sam beat her to it. She'd been on tenterhooks ever since last night. If it was bad news concerning Grover Cleveland or Collette, he wanted to be the one to break it to her. He listened, frowning thoughtfully at what he heard.

"That was the police," he said, replacing the receiver.

"What did they want? Do they have news about Grover Cleveland and Collette?"

"They didn't say. The sergeant just asked if I could stop by today."

"I'll come with you."

Sam shook his head. "Not today. You're going to see the dentist, remember?" He smiled at her pout. Going to the dentist was something Carla put off as long as possible. She'd already postponed the appointment three times, using every excuse she could think of. During the months they'd been married, he'd discovered she dreaded going to both doctors and dentists. This time he'd made the appointment for her. And he wasn't allowing her to wiggle out of it.

After making sure she left in time for her appointment, Sam headed to the precinct station. Inside, the air was thick with smoke. The squad room reeked of disinfectant, which failed to cover the underlying odors of sweat, stale coffee, and something Sam decided was best left unidentified. He gave his name to the duty officer and was told to take a seat.

"Sergeant Nichols will be with you shortly."

Sergeant Nichols, a slight, wiry man with thinning hair, appeared a few minutes later. After introducing himself, he gestured at Sam to follow him to a small room down the hall.

Sam spared a moment to look around, his glance taking in muddy green walls and scarred linoleum floor. A narrow table and two hard-backed chairs didn't encourage comfort. A mirror, probably two way, covered one wall.

"Glad you could make it, Mr. Hastings," Nichols said as he flipped through a pile of papers with nicotine-stained fingers.

"Thanks for calling. Have you found the dogs?"

"No. But we got a call last night that I thought you might be interested in."

"Someone else's dog has been stolen?"

"Not dog. Dogs. And cats and rabbits and white mice." The sergeant laughed, obviously enjoying the expression on Sam's face. "A pet store was broken into. Strange thing was, the cash register wasn't touched. But all the animals were gone. And a couple of dozen sacks of food."

"You think the incidents are related?"

Sergeant Nichols scratched his head. "Could be. I don't hold much with coincidences."

Neither did Sam.

He repeated the conversation to Carla when he returned home that evening.

"Maybe we've been on the wrong track altogether."

"Who'd want a bunch of animals?" she asked. "None of them are worth much. It's not like they're pedigreed or breeders. They're just people's pets."

"Animal labs," Sam said, thinking out loud. "You know, cosmetic firms, medical research, that kind of thing." He watched as she turned a peculiar shade of green. He wrapped an arm around her waist and helped her to the sofa. "Are you all right?"

"I think so." She drew a shaky breath. "It's just the thought of someone using Collette and Grover Cleveland for — experiments."

"Yeah. I know." He studied her face. Her color was returning to normal, but she still looked pale. "How did the appointment go?"

She made a face.

"That bad?"

"I've got a cavity. He said I should've come in six months ago."

Sam struggled to look properly sympathetic. "So when are you going back?"

"Next week." She grimaced. "Maybe I'll stop down at the Pet Palace tomorrow and see if Jerry Foster heard anything. He knows just about all the pets in the area. He might be able to tell us if any others are missing."

"Good idea."

The Pet Palace had occupied the corner of Saratoga's main street for more than forty years, according to Mrs. Miller, the church's most reliable gossip. Jerry Foster had managed the store for the last twenty of those years after taking over from his father.

Jerry shook his head as he swept up a spilled bag of dog food. "I'm sorry, Reverend Hastings. I haven't heard anything. I wish I could tell you something that would help."

"Thanks anyway." She glanced around the small store, with its flimsy locks and old-fashioned sash windows. "You heard about that pet store being robbed?"

"I heard all right." He frowned. "Hey, you don't think they're related, do you? The robbery and the missing pets?"

She shrugged. "Your guess is as good as mine."

"Doesn't seem to make sense — a bunch of dogs and cats being stolen."

She repeated Sam's theory that the animals had been stolen for medical research, shuddering at the grisly pictures it painted in her mind.

"Medical research?" Jerry looked thoughtful. "I hate to say it, but I think the councilman's off base."

"Could be. We're just trying to check out all the possibilities."

"Yeah."

"You'll be careful, won't you, Jerry? If we're right, your store could be hit too."

"Sure thing, Reverend. I'll keep everything buttoned up tight." He grinned. "How's George doing?"

"Eating us out of house and home."

"Didn't I tell you?"

"You sure did."

She was smiling as she left the store. Jerry was a good friend to pet owners. He could diagnose most common pet ailments with just a few questions and suggest the best foods for different breeds of dogs and cats. He was generally knowledgeable about behavior problems. When she was trying to train George to stop barking at every car that passed, she'd called him with a question more than once.

She'd forgotten to mention that they'd added a new member to the family. She chuckled, remembering Thomas' indignation this morning when they refused to let him bring his latest catch of the day — a large rat — inside. He'd started supplementing store-bought food with the occasional mouse or rat. He'd gotten even with them, though, by dropping the rat on the front doorstep. Much to her relief, Sam had disposed of the thing.

At home, she contemplated what she was about to do. She spent the next few hours first talking herself out of it and then convincing herself she had to do it.

"What do you think, Thomas?"

Thomas had been sunning himself in the bay window of her bedroom. He opened an eye, stretched, and regarded her lazily. Apparently considering her unworthy of further attention, he placed a paw over his eyes and resumed his nap.

"Fine friend you are," she grumbled. "You won't even listen when I'm telling you my troubles."

A purred sigh was the only response.

"Sam's so stubborn, he won't even listen. If he'd just give them a chance . . ."

Thomas blinked and then yawned widely.

"If I go ahead with this, I'm asking for trouble," she told him. "But if I don't, Sam and his parents may never make up. I *have* to do something."

Only once before had she brought up the subject of his parents — five months ago at Christmas. She'd suggested they invite them over for Christmas dinner.

"It's a time for families," she had said.

Sam had drawn her into his arms. "*You're* all the family I need. You and Ethan and Maude."

"But —"

"Drop it, Carla. Please."

She'd done as he asked because she couldn't bear to tarnish their first Christmas together with harsh words. But she wasn't willing to give up on the idea of establishing some kind of relationship with Sam's parents. If Sam was too stubborn to take the first step, then it was up to her.

"He'll thank me when he thinks about it," she said.

Thomas opened his other eye. From his position on the window ledge, he gave her a haughty look as if to say he knew better.

She paced back and forth. "Maybe a small dinner party . . . just the four of us."

The larger cat jumped down from his perch and sashayed between her legs.

She barely caught herself from falling over him. "Sam's right. You are a nuisance."

Thomas maintained a dignified silence.

"All right, all right," she grumbled. "I know you didn't mean to trip me. Come on. I suppose all this talk about dinner parties is making you hungry."

Thomas led the way to the kitchen, where she filled his dish with canned cat food. He meowed plaintively.

"Absolutely not. No salmon tonight. You and George eat better than Sam and I do as it is."

After darting a reproachful look at her, Thomas began to eat. Carla watched him, wondering why everything couldn't be solved as easily.

"Nothing ventured, nothing gained," she muttered and picked up the phone.

Five minutes later, she recradled the

receiver, praying she hadn't just made the biggest mistake of her life.

"You what?" Sam asked an hour later as he helped her set the table.

"I invited your parents for dinner. Friday night. Around seven."

"Uninvite them."

Although she'd been prepared for his resistance to the idea, the flat tone of the command and the coldness in his eyes frightened her. His voice was quiet. Too quiet. She would feel better if he screamed or yelled or something. Anything but this deadly calm.

"Sam, they sounded pleased — really pleased — that I called. Please, for me."

He turned away. "No."

"Won't you even see them?"

"I haven't talked to my parents, except about the campaign, in the last five years. I don't see any reason to start now."

"That's every reason to start now. They're your parents, Sam. Doesn't that mean anything?"

He turned to her. The naked pain in his eyes made her take his hand, but he shrugged her away.

"My parents aren't like yours," he said. "My mother's idea of a family supper is a

catered dinner for thirty of her most inti-
mate friends. My father can't sit down for
two minutes without a phone in his ear,
checking on the market."

"Then this will be change for them."

"You don't get it, do you? They don't want
to change. I spent the first twenty years of
my life trying to get them to change."

She heard the anguish in his voice, a pain
he probably wasn't even aware of. And she
ached for him because of it.

"They're your parents, Sam. They love
you."

"They don't know the meaning of the
word."

"Maybe it's time they learned."

"You can't teach love, Carla. Not to
people like them."

"They need you in their lives. They may
not show it, but they miss you."

"They've never missed me. Do you know
how I spent Christmas before I was old
enough to go to boarding school? With the
maid. While they went off to Europe. Or St.
Croix. Or New Zealand. Wherever was hot
that year. They never even bothered to ask
if I wanted to go."

"And when you were older?"

"I stayed by myself." He gave her a hard

look. "I liked it that way. I still like it that way."

"Give them a chance, Sam. People change."

"Not them."

"How do you know unless you talk to them?"

"Stay out of my life."

"I thought I was part of your life," she said quietly.

"You are."

"Just not this part? Is that it, Sam? I can be part of your life, but only the parts that are easy? The parts that don't require you to open up or take risks? The parts that you decide to allow me into?"

"That's not what I mean."

"Yes." She brushed his cheek. "I'm afraid you do."

He turned and walked out.

He ran as if trying to race the wind. In reality, his thoughts were far more difficult to outrun. They churned around in his head with the fury of a whirlpool, swirling, spinning, spiraling out of control. He slowed as he felt a faint stitch in his side.

Carla. Carla. Her name pounded in his head in rhythm to the pounding of his feet on the pavement.

He slowed even more, his breath coming

in harsh gasps, the cramp in his side now a raging pain. He couldn't outdistance his anger. Or his fear. His anger faded almost immediately. He knew Carla was only trying to help him come to terms with his parents. But his fear grew. Fear of facing the past. He'd spent the better part of his adult life trying to forget it. Could he now open that up, probe his feelings, and survive?

Overriding that fear was an even greater one. Fear that he'd lost Carla. How could she live with him after the ugly words he'd hurled at her? How could he live with himself?

The thought caused him to stop completely. He looked around, not recognizing his surroundings. How far had he run? Obviously not far enough to outdistance his thoughts. Leaning forward, he braced his hands on his knees, inhaling deeply.

He needed to see Carla. Needed to know she was still there. He ignored the sharpening pain in his side as he headed home.

Home. It wasn't place, but a person. Carla. She was his touchstone, his anchor. Without her there was no reason to get up in the morning. Without her there was no reason for anything.

So great was his need to see her that he

opened the door with more force than necessary.

She wasn't there.

He knew it even before calling her name and waiting. He knew it without seeing the mournful expression in George's eyes. He knew it without hearing the accusing hiss Thomas directed at him. He knew it because the essence that was Carla was missing — the scent of her hair, the sound of her laughter, the sweetness of her smile. All that — and more — were gone.

And he had no one to blame but himself.

Carla cradled the baby to her as he finished the last of his bottle. "You're growing so much, your mommy and daddy won't even recognize you when they come to visit tonight."

At four pounds and eight ounces, Dustin Pratt had nearly doubled his birth weight. The feeding tubes had been removed, and he could now take a bottle — a major accomplishment for a baby who hadn't been expected to live.

He nuzzled her cheek, and she cuddled him closer.

"I'll tell you a secret," she whispered. "If you keep this up, you can blow this joint pretty soon."

He yawned widely.

"Okay, okay. I get the message. After that big meal, you're ready for a nap. Am I right?"

He yawned again.

"But first we need to change your diaper." She unfastened the tapes of the doll-sized diaper, scooted it out from under him, and replaced it with a clean one. "There." She disposed of the soiled diaper in a waste bin.

Dustin searched for his fist, found it, and began to suck noisily.

She snuggled him to her, settled in the ICU nursery's rocking chair, and began humming a lullaby, one her mother had sung to her. A tiny smile touched Dustin's lips as his eyes closed. She'd never believed the old lore that claimed a baby's smile was only gas. Babies were incredibly responsive creatures, sensitive to every nuance and feeling. They didn't need words to understand love. They needed only their hearts.

A tear trickled down her cheek. If only adults could be equally as smart.

A short while later, Sam found her in the rocking chair.

He stood quietly, not wanting to disturb her. Her hair fell around her face, casting her face in shadow. She rocked gently, murmuring all the while. He tried to catch the words, but he could only make out broken syllables. But he caught the message.

Love.

The kind of love that Carla gave to everyone.

And he'd almost thrown it away with his pig-headedness and pride. Tears pricked his eyes as he savored the picture she made with the baby nestled to her.

He listened to the infant's soft mewling as he snuggled deeper into her arms. A sweet peace wrapped its way around his heart as he pictured her holding *their* child, suckling the baby at her breast. Someday the picture would become reality. For now, he needed to make things right with the woman who was life and light to him.

He waited as she returned the baby to the nurse, removed her gown, and walked out of the nursery. "How did you know to find me here?" she asked quietly.

"I didn't. I took a chance."

"I'm glad," she said softly.

"So am I." He hesitated. "I'm sorry."

She looked up. "I know."

There was no reproach in her eyes, no recrimination in her voice, only acceptance. Once more he was humbled — and shamed.

"I . . . I was wrong." The words weren't as

difficult to say as he'd feared. And with them he shed the last of the pain, a legacy of his childhood.

"It's all right," she said, trailing her fingers along his cheek.

He caught them and brought them to his lips, kissing the tip of each finger in turn. "What did I ever do to deserve you?" he murmured.

"You love me. Just like I love you. That's all it takes."

He looked into the soft warmth of her eyes and knew she meant every word. Carla didn't ration out her love, she gave it as naturally as she breathed. He'd thought he understood that; now he realized he was only beginning to see the full magnitude of what it meant to be loved by her.

Before Carla became part of his life, he'd assumed everyone doled out love and approval as his parents had — with stingy hands and cold hearts. But Carla had introduced him to a new way of loving — and living.

He didn't want to go back to the old way, where love was a commodity and approval was given or withheld depending on the whim of others. His thoughts took him full circle. His parents. He searched Carla's face, wondering why he'd thought he had to hide this part of himself from her. Perhaps it was shame. Or pride. Or some twisted combination of the two. He chose his words carefully, needing to understand as much as to explain. Only then could he ask for her forgiveness.

"My parents and I have been strangers for as long as I can remember. I'd convinced myself I wanted it that way. But now, I'm not sure." The words caught in his throat, but he managed to get them out. "I'm afraid."

"Maybe they are too."

He started to deny it. His father afraid? The idea intrigued him. His father, as he proudly told anyone in earshot, was a self-made man who'd earned his money the hard way. He'd fought his way out of poverty by the sheer force of his will. Sam couldn't imagine his father afraid of anything or anyone. Least of all his son.

And his mother? Sam frowned, trying to remember when he'd last seen his mother display any emotion at all.

"Your mother's really very shy," Carla said.

He looked at her with undisguised skepticism. "You've talked to her once. What makes you think she's shy?"

"I could hear it in her voice."

Sam didn't doubt it. Carla could tell more about a person by just listening than most people could after a lengthy friendship.

"She doesn't know how to relate to you," Carla said. "If you gave her a chance, you might be surprised."

He thought about it. His mother was on the board of a half dozen charities. Invitations to her dinner parties were among the most sought after in the city.

"Give them a chance, Sam. That's all I'm asking. Give yourself a chance. People change."

She was right. He was proof of it. But he hadn't done it on his own. It had taken Carla and a hard look at his life to turn him around. Maybe his parents needed the same kind of help. Maybe he was the one who could do it. Maybe . . . A smile rested on his lips. Carla was doing it again. Making him believe in miracles.

He took her hand. "Let's go home."

Her hand curled inside his. "I thought you'd never ask."

The days swirled together, racing to Friday. His anxiety grew in inverse proportion to the time remaining before the dinner party.

Changing into a fresh shirt before his parents were due to arrive, Sam eyed

Thomas, who was making himself at home on Sam's dresser.

"You plan on making an appearance tonight?"

Thomas meowed, a sound Sam took to be a yes.

"Well, just mind your manners, okay? No sneaking food from the table."

Thomas' sniff was so humanly disdainful that Sam grinned and felt his tension beginning to fade. Maybe tonight wouldn't be so bad after all.

"What do you think?" he addressed the cat, holding up two ties. "The blue or the gray?"

Thomas swatted at the blue one with his paw.

"The blue it is."

Lately he'd taken to talking to Thomas as if the cat were a lifelong friend instead of a recent addition to the household. This from a man who had considered the yellow-eyed cat a menace just a few weeks ago. Come to think of it, he talked to George the same way. Six months ago, he would have scoffed at anyone who talked to their pets. The funny thing was, how he didn't find it strange.

He frowned. Maybe that was strange in itself. Of course, his whole life had taken a strange course when he'd married Carla. Suddenly he smiled, deciding *strange* wasn't so bad after all. Not when it meant having Carla in his life.

He couldn't bear to think about the alternative.

"George, get down," Sam ordered. George had just jumped on his father, covering the charcoal gray Savile Row suit with dog hair. It didn't bode well for the rest of the evening.

"He's all right." Gerald Hastings knelt by George's side to rub the dog's neck. "My old man never let us have a pet. Another mouth to feed. I never let on, but I spent most of my paper route money feeding a stray that used to come around." He stood, brushing the hair from his slacks.

Sam noticed the slight flush on his father's cheeks. He had never known him to be embarrassed by anything before. He caught Carla watching him and felt his own cheeks turn warm under her gaze. He was doing this for her, he reminded himself. There was no law saying he had to like his parents; all he had to do was get along with them for an evening. He could do that much.

Thomas wandered in, surveyed the room with his usual air of disdain, and settled himself under George's nose. George placed a huge paw on the cat's back.

"Darndest thing I've ever seen," Gerald said. "Doesn't he know he's a cat?"

Sam had often wondered the same thing. His lips twitched. A rumbling sound made him look at his father in amazement. The older man was laughing, with tears streaming down his cheeks.

"Don't know what got in me," Gerald said.

Sam didn't know either. Whatever it was, though, had softened the hard-edged veneer his father had always worn like a suit of armor. To Sam's knowledge, his father rarely smiled, much less laughed. He sipped his glass of wine, hoping the red Burgundy would restore his equilibrium.

His mother opened up when Carla mentioned the church was holding a bazaar to raise money for the homeless shelter.

"How much do you hope to make?"

"A couple of thousand dollars, if we're lucky."

"Oh, we can do a lot better than that," Jeanette Hastings said.

"We?"

Jeanette flushed. "I'd like to help — if you'll let me."

Sam stared at her until Carla gently kicked

him under the table. He'd never known his mother to offer her help to any cause that wasn't approved by the social lions. His gaze strayed to Carla. The smile she gave him in return was all the answer he needed.

He shouldn't have been surprised. He already knew the spell she wove over those who came into contact with her. A magical spell of love. He sat back to watch a miracle take place.

"I'd like that, Mrs. Hastings," Carla said softly. "I'd like that very much. We could use someone with your experience."

His mother looked pleased. "Please, dear. Call me Jeanette."

They spent the rest of the dinner discussing various fund-raising ideas. Sam listened in amazement as his mother gave surprisingly sharp insights. By the end of the evening, he had mellowed enough to start seeing his parents in a new way.

The feeling lasted until Gerald threw a sharp look Carla's way and asked, "Are you some kind of magician, young lady?"

"She's a minister," Sam said stiffly.

"I know that." Gerald gave his son a level look. "And she's got us talking like a family should for the first time in years. I'd say that qualifies her as a magician."

Sam flushed. His father was right. Carla

had accomplished what neither he nor his parents had been able to.

"And I thank heaven for it," Jeanette said, reaching up to brush her lips against Sam's cheek.

Sam felt as if he'd wandered into another dimension. He couldn't remember the last time his mother had kissed him. Sometime around his eighth birthday, he thought.

They'd barely said good-bye when Carla turned and threw her arms around him. "Thank you."

Automatically his arms closed around her. "No, thank *you*." He curled his hands over her shoulders and put enough distance between them so he could see her face. Maybe his father was right — maybe she *was* a magician, Sam reflected. How else could he explain what had happened this evening? "How do you do it?" He saw the bewilderment in her eyes as she looked up at him. It was genuine, he knew. She had no idea what she'd accomplished.

"Do what?"

"Never mind," he said, drawing her to him once more. "I love you."

"I know. Just like I love you."

It was that simple. And that complicated. Love. A four letter word that had changed his life. That and a very special woman.

"Did you see your father with George?" she asked. "He was like a little boy with his first dog."

Sam nodded, the image lodged in his mind. For years he'd tried to find some common ground with his parents before eventually giving up. All it had taken was an overly friendly dog. And Carla.

Always Carla.

"Your parents need to learn how to love," she said. "We can teach them." Linking her hands around his neck, she pulled his head down until their lips touched.

There was no better teacher around, he thought.

Chapter Three

The following morning Thelma Harvey summoned Carla for a visit. Carla groaned. So far they'd made no progress in finding Grover Cleveland. She dreaded giving the old lady the bad news. As annoying as Thelma could be, Carla cared about her.

"I'll be back in a couple of hours," she told Sam as she ran a brush through her hair.

"You want me to go with you?"

She shook her head. "I'll be fine. But thanks for the offer."

When she rang the doorbell of the restored Victorian house, a sandy-haired young man answered it. He held out his hand. "Martin Clark."

Her brow furrowed momentarily as she tried to place the name.

"Thelma's my grandmother," he said, holding the door open as she walked inside.

She smiled. "Of course. Thelma's told me

a lot about you." Automatically she headed toward the small room off the kitchen, where Thelma usually entertained company. But Martin gestured to a closed door. Her smile deepened as he led her into the old-fashioned parlor. Obviously Thelma considered the visit important. Only a select few were ever invited into the "good room."

"My grandmother's spoken of you often, Reverend Hastings," he said.

"Some good, I hope," she said, carefully perching on the edge of a velvet settee.

Martin sat down on a wingback chair. He appeared to choose his words carefully. "She's not an easy person to please."

They shared an understanding smile. Carla found herself liking Martin. She could see why Thelma doted on him.

"Your grandmother's very proud of you."

"Too proud," he said with a wry smile.

"Here we are." Thelma bustled into the room, carrying a silver tray laden with a teapot, china, and a plate of scones. "Have you two been getting acquainted?" she asked, handing delicate cups and saucers to Carla and Martin. "I wanted two of my favorite people to get to know each other."

Carla raised her eyebrow. She was hardly one of Thelma Harvey's favorite people. The older woman made a habit of pointing out

Carla's failings, especially in church. Carla put up with it because she understood Thelma's desire to feel needed.

She glanced at Martin and found him grinning at her over his grandmother's head.

"Martin's promised to help look for Grover Cleveland. He's very smart, you know. Martin, that is." Mrs. Harvey looked momentarily flustered. "Not that Grover Cleveland isn't intelligent also. In a dog way."

Carla bit her lip, trying to keep her laughter from bubbling out.

"Not all dogs are as intelligent as my Grover Cleveland, though." The older woman lowered her voice. "The Millers' Collette is nothing but a hussy. She entices him to . . . visit." The last word was said with a delicate shudder.

This time Carla wasn't as successful in suppressing her laughter. She quickly covered it with a fit of coughing.

Thelma threw her a sharp look. Apparently satisfied with what she saw on Carla's face, she cast a fond smile at her grandson. "Did I tell you that Martin graduated from high school when he was only sixteen years old? He worked nights to put himself through college."

Carla tried to appear as if she were hearing the story for the first time. Martin sent her a sympathetic look, obviously aware of his grandmother's fondness for bragging about him.

"Gram, you're embarrassing me," he muttered when she gave no indication of stopping.

Thelma gave him an indulgent smile. "You're too modest. He always has been," she confided to Carla. "I tell him that he ought to go out more, find a young lady and settle down, but he's all wrapped up in his studies."

"I'm in med school, Gram. I don't have time to date, even if I did have the money."

Carla decided it was time to intervene. "We hope you'll be joining us for our church fair this year, Martin."

"My schedule's a little unsettled right now." At Thelma's frown, he added, "But if I'm here, I'll be sure to come."

"Of course he'll come," Thelma said. "Having Martin visit is like a ray of sunshine. If only Grover Cleveland . . ." She turned a watery smile on Carla. "Of course I've appreciated all you've done, Reverend Hastings, but family is so important at a time like this, don't you think?"

"Very important."

"That's why I'm so glad Martin's here. It

makes the loss so much more bearable. If I didn't have him, why, I don't know what I'd do."

"It's all right, Gram," Martin said, leaning over to kiss Thelma's cheek. "I'm here for as long as you need me."

She patted his hand. "You're a good boy." She dabbed at her eyes before turning her attention back to Carla. "Well, Reverend, we won't keep you. I know you have a full schedule."

Carla placed her cup on the saucer and stood. Apparently she was being dismissed. Once more she exchanged a wry smile with Martin.

"I'll see you both on Sunday," she said.

Armed with scrub brushes and rags, Carla set out the last of her cleaning supplies. Polishing the chapel pews was one of her favorite activities. After much persuading, she'd convinced Mr. Porter, the church custodian, to allow her to perform the chore. Something about seeing the wood shine as a result of her efforts always lifted her spirits. It was as if she could rub away all the ugliness and grime in the world and replace them with something beautiful and clean. It was fanciful, she knew, but the image stuck. She attacked a piece of dried-on gum.

Today she'd invited Jared Walker to help her. She smiled, remembering how he'd come into their lives last winter. Sam had volunteered for Project Reach-Out, an organization that paired troubled youths with adult mentors. Sullen and defiant, Jared had been matched with Sam, daring him to be his friend. It hadn't taken long for Sam to tear down the barriers the boy had erected around himself, making Jared a part of their lives.

She heard a scuffling behind her and turned around.

Jared, dressed in grubby jeans and a ragged sweat-shirt, stood in the door, hands shoved into his pockets.

"Hi. Ready to help clean benches?" she asked.

"Sure."

"I think I've got all the stuff right here. . . ." She let the rest of the sentence go unfinished as she saw how he shifted his gaze away from her. "Something the matter?"

"Uh, Carla . . ." He stopped, looking more ill at ease than she could remember.

"What is it?" she asked gently.

"Nothing," he muttered, picking up a rag

and starting to polish the area she'd just completed.

Gently she took the rag from him and gestured for him to sit down. "Spill it," she ordered with mock ferocity.

"It's this guy I met. At school."

She smiled encouragingly.

"His name's Ron Franks. Everybody calls him Stick because he's so skinny. We . . . uh . . . sit next to each other in art class. We sort of got to be friends." Jared hesitated. "He's really good with paint. Spray paint."

She waited.

"He does fancy lettering with spray paint." He looked at her anxiously.

"He spray paints. That's great. Maybe he can help us with the posters for the dance —" She stopped abruptly. "Did you say he does fancy lettering with spray paints?" She quelled her sense of foreboding. Lots of kids liked to use spray paint. There was no reason to believe that Ron was the person who had vandalized the church last winter. No reason, except for the way Jared avoided her eyes.

"We got to talking — like guys do, you know."

Carla held her breath, somehow knowing what was coming and still praying she was wrong.

"He said he'd made some bread a few months back when he did a job at a church."

"No . . ." The word caught in her throat.

"It was Ron," Jared said, confirming her fears.

She let her glance circle the chapel where she'd already arranged flowers for Sunday's service. Beautifully painted scenes depicting stories from the Bible covered the walls. Jared had done the work last January when the church had been vandalized, the walls splashed with ugly obscenities.

"He feels real bad about what he did. He only did it because his mom's welfare check was late and some guy offered him a pile of money."

Tony. Carla closed her eyes, remembering the threats the thug had made against her last winter as part of a plot to prevent a community home from being built in an abandoned warehouse. Tony Owens hadn't been behind the plot; he was only the henchman. And he'd used Ron in his twisted plan.

"Ron and his mom were practically starving," Jared said, bringing her back to the present. "He didn't want to do it."

She swallowed hard, trying to digest what Jared had just told her. Images of red and black letters spelling out vicious threats swirled around in her head. Nightmares about the ugly words had plagued her for weeks afterward.

"Why are you telling me this?"

"I thought maybe you'd want to know."

"There's more, isn't there?"

He nodded miserably. "Ron's been in trouble at school ever since he — ever since it happened. I think he's been beating himself up over what he did."

"What do you want me to do?" But she didn't need Jared to tell her what to do. She knew the answer. She just wasn't sure she could do it.

She spent that night praying for strength to do what she knew was right. By the following day, she was ready.

She dialed Jared's number. "Can you bring Ron by the house after school today?" she asked.

"Uh . . . sure."

Shortly after four, she pulled a pan of cookies from the oven. The aroma of chocolate chip cookies filled the kitchen.

Despite her calm, she jumped when the doorbell rang. A deep breath restored her composure. When she opened the kitchen door, she managed a smile for the two boys.

"Carla, uh, Reverend Hastings, this is Stick . . . I mean, uh . . . Ron Franks. Ron, this is Carla Hastings."

Carla hid a smile as Jared stumbled over the introductions. She switched her attention to the other boy. Dressed in Army boots, camouflage pants, and a khaki T-shirt, Ron Franks had done his best to look tough and hard. He slouched against a wall, not bothering to hold out his hand. Obviously he meant his stance to be intimidating. Carla found it more pathetic than alarming.

She held out her hand. "Glad to meet you, Ron."

"Yeah. You too," he mumbled.

She looked at this boy who'd caused her so much pain. For months she'd struggled with her feelings toward the person who'd vandalized the church, trying to find it in herself to forgive him. Now he was here in her home. Suddenly she no longer saw a boy who'd painted monstrous words across the walls of the chapel, but a scared child who needed her.

Ron shuffled from foot to foot, clearly uneasy.

Her empathy for others flared to life, melting away the last of her anger. She gestured to the kitchen table and they all sat down. "Jared says you two met in art class at school."

"Yeah. That's right. I . . . uh . . . I like to

mess around with paints." He blushed bright pink.

Carla thought of the warnings Ron had spray painted on the walls of the church. Even at the time, she'd noticed the intricacy of the designs, the talent behind the ugly images.

"Ron's real good with watercolors too," Jared rushed in.

"I'm not bad," Ron muttered.

Jared pulled out a folder. "Look at this." He opened the folder to show a mountain scene.

"May I?" Carla asked.

With a glance at Ron, Jared passed the picture to her.

She studied the detail of the delicately tinted picture. "It's beautiful."

Ron's blush deepened. "It's nothing."

"You've got real talent, Ron."

"You really think so?"

She smiled at the eagerness in his voice. "I know so. The question is, what are you going to do with it?"

He shrugged.

"Have you thought about art school after you graduate?"

"Oh, yeah. I think about that all the time. Me and my mom got so much money that we're on welfare." He sneered. "You planning on being my fairy godmother or something?"

"I'd like to help you," she said quietly. "But whether or not you go to art school or college or anywhere else is up to you."

"In case you haven't heard, lady, that kind of junk takes money."

"So get a job."

He flicked her a contemptuous glance. "How many people you know gonna hire a JD?"

"JD?"

"Juvenile delinquent," Jared translated.

She focused her attention back on Ron. "Is that what you are?"

"That's what *they* say I am."

"Who's they?"

He gestured vaguely. "You know. They. The school. Social workers. Everybody."

She cocked her head to one side. "Funny. You don't look like the kind of guy who lets other people pin a label on him. Of course, I *could* be wrong."

Ron glared at her. "I don't let no one do nothing to me unless I say so."

"So prove it."

The surprise on the boy's face was almost comical. "How?"

"Come to work for me."

"You?"

"Me."

"Why?"

"Because I could use someone with your talents."

"What talents are you talking about?"

She took his hands in hers and turned them over, palms up. They were covered with nicks and scratches, dried paint, and india ink. "The talents that got you these."

Ron followed her gaze. "You want me to paint something for you?"

"The church youth group —"

"I ain't teaching no snotty-nosed brats how to hold a brush."

"I'm not asking you to," she returned evenly.

"Then what's the deal?"

"The church youth group needs to raise some money to buy new equipment for the recreational hall. We're sponsoring a dance."

"So?"

"We need someone to do some knock-'em-dead posters to advertise the event."

"You want me to do posters?"

"Is there a problem with that?"

"I'm an artist, lady. Not a sign painter."

Jared, who had been silent up until now, laid a hand on his friend's arm. "Hey, man, it's a chance to make some bread. Carla, I mean the reverend's all right. If she hires you to do a job, she'll treat you fair."

The belligerence on Ron's face faded to uncertainty as he lifted his gaze to meet hers.

She saw the warring emotions: hope and fear mixed in with a healthy dose of pride.

"There's something you ought to know," he said, sliding her an embarrassed glance.

She waited.

"I trashed the church last winter." A flush stained the boy's cheeks.

"I know."

"You do?" He turned an accusing gaze on Jared.

"I had to tell her," Jared said.

"Yeah. I guess you did." Ron turned back to Carla. "My mom and me, we're on our own. Sometime things get rough, like when her welfare check doesn't come on time. When a dude offered me a couple of hundred dollars to — you know — I took it." He lowered his head, obviously ashamed of his part in the vandalism. It was, she suspected, the closest to an apology as she was likely to get.

She took a deep breath, praying she could find the right words. "You did what you felt you had to for you and your mom. I'm not going to pretend that I like what you did.

But I understand why you felt you had to do it."

"You still gonna hire me?"

"I'm still gonna hire you."

"Let's talk turkey." He cocked a brow, giving her a considering look. "You know something?"

"What?"

"You're not bad."

"For a preacher lady?" She held out the plate of cookies.

"Yeah." He grinned and picked up a couple of cookies. "For a preacher lady."

"You did what?" Sam asked as she set the table for dinner. He placed the silverware on the table, praying he hadn't heard correctly, even while knowing he had.

"I hired Ron Franks to do some posters for the church dance."

He rubbed the back of his neck. Jared had already filled him in on Ron. "Let me get this straight. You hired the boy who trashed the church last winter to do posters for a dance?"

She nodded. "It's perfect. He needs a job, we need sensational posters. What could be better?"

He could think of a lot of things. He was about to tell her so when he saw the happiness shining in her eyes. Whatever he thought about the boy who'd vandalized the church, he couldn't deny Carla the opportunity to do what she did best: love others.

Still, he closed his hands over her shoulders and shook her gently, part in frustration, part in indulgence. The battle was lost, and he hadn't even gotten a chance to fire his first shot. Sadly the experience was a familiar one since he'd met Carla.

"You're sure you want to do this?" He had to try once more.

"I'm sure." She reached up to kiss his cheek. "He only vandalized the church because he and his mom were broke. He'd never have done it otherwise. Besides, he wants to make up for his actions."

"He said that?"

"Not in so many words," she hedged. "But I could see it in his eyes." She looked up at him, her own eyes huge and appealing. "How can we deny him the chance to prove it?"

Sam folded his arms around her, resting his chin on top of her head. He knew when he'd been outmaneuvered by Carla. Still, he couldn't completely quell the uneasy feeling that settled in the pit of his stomach.

No matter how much Carla told him Ron

Franks had changed, he couldn't stop remembering the pain the boy had caused her. He couldn't forget the desolation in her eyes when she saw the obscenities splashed across the walls of the church. He couldn't forget the blame she'd shouldered because she felt she'd caused the attack on the church. Even knowing her as he did, he marveled that she could forgive the boy who'd desecrated something she held so dear. Not only had she forgiven him but she'd offered him a job as well.

"When is he going to start?"

"Saturday. We decided he'd do the work at the church. He'll meet me here."

He nodded, mentally rearranging his day. He couldn't stop her from giving the boy a job, but he could be there just to make sure . . . He didn't finish the thought, feeling disloyal to Carla when she so obviously believed in Ron. Sam wanted to share that belief. But years of cynicism had left him skeptical about such a complete about-face.

She reached up to touch his cheek. "Are you angry with me?"

"No." He could never be angry with her for being what she was. But neither could he stand by and do nothing when he felt she was in danger of being hurt. His mouth turned grim. Ron Franks didn't know it, but come Saturday they were going to have a little talk. In the meantime, Sam did the only thing he could. He gathered her to him, holding her close and praying she wouldn't be hurt. "You're amazing."

"I know. How else would I put up with you?" Her soft laugh wrapped its way around him, suffusing him with warmth.

The tension inside him eased, and he laughed with her.

On Saturday morning, Sam suggested Carla go to the church and set things up while he waited for Ron. When the bell rang, he opened the door and gave himself a moment to study the boy standing before him.

Ron was tall, thin, and gangly. His clothes were worn but clean; his long hair was drawn back into a ponytail at the nape of his neck. A single gold hoop adorned one ear.

Sam held out his hand. "Sam Hastings."

"Stick — I mean, Ron Franks."

"I hear you're going to do some posters for the church dance."

"Yeah." Ron cocked a hip against the door frame. "Got a problem with that?"

"No problem," Sam said easily. "Just some advice. Carla believes in you. Don't let her down."

Ron straightened and assumed a belligerent stance. "I keep my word."

"Glad to hear it. Come on. She's waiting at the church for you."

Once they reached the church, Ron stopped outside, turning to face Sam. "You don't like me."

"I don't know you."

"Don't play word games with me. I ain't dumb. I know when someone thinks I'm dirt."

"Carla believes in you," Sam said evenly. "That's enough for me."

"What's with her anyway? She some kind of do-gooder?"

A half smile touched Sam's lips as he remembered that Jared had used the same words when he asked Sam why he volunteered at Project Reach-Out. "She sees something special in you." Now that he'd met the boy, he was beginning to understand. Ron had an engaging quality that was hard to resist. Still, Sam intended to reserve judgment.

Ron scowled. "I ain't some project that she can practice her do-gooding stuff on."

Sam ignored that. "Let me ask you something."

The boy lifted a brow.

"Why are you here?"

Ron gave him a disbelieving look. "You crazy, man? She promised me bread."

"That's all?"

"You better believe it." But his tone lacked conviction.

Sam didn't comment. When Ron started inside the church, Sam curled his hand over the boy's shoulder. "You're here because Carla believes in you."

"So?"

"You hurt her once. Do it again and you'll regret it."

"Who's gonna make me?"

Sam didn't bother answering. He just continued to stare at Ron until the boy looked away.

"Okay, man. No sweat. I ain't gonna hurt her."

"Then there's no problem."

"That's right." Ron looked relieved. "No problem. No problem at all."

"Good. One more thing."

"Yeah?"

"You weren't alone when you trashed the church." It wasn't a question, and Ron didn't treat it as such.

"No. I wasn't alone. But I'm not giving up my buddies."

Sam respected the boy's unflinching honesty. And his loyalty, however misplaced. He was beginning to understand what Carla saw in Ron, this boy who rubbed uncomfortably against the edges of adulthood — no longer a child, but not yet full grown. Ron was at a crossroads in his life. Maybe, Sam reflected, he and Carla could help him take a right turn.

Four hours later, Sam had to hand it to Ron. The posters drying on the classroom table sparkled with originality and imagination.

"They're wonderful," Carla said, throwing her arms around Ron and hugging him.

He pulled away, looking embarrassed but pleased. "They're nothing special." But his gaze sought Sam's.

"Don't sell yourself short," Sam said. "You've got real talent."

"I'm going to hang this one up right now," Carla said, pointing to a particularly bright sign done in primary colors. "But first things first." She opened her purse and handed a couple of bills to Ron. "Thanks again."

Sam saw the boy's eyes widen at the amount.

"Jeez."

She smiled. "Can I call you again if I need some more posters?"

"Uh, sure. That'd be great."

Sam noticed how Ron kept his gaze trained on Carla as she gathered up the posters.

"Why did she do it?" he asked after she left. "Give me a job and all. Most people won't give me the time of day, and she tells me she'll pay me to do a few signs. She's even gonna talk to my art teacher, see if I can get extra credit for this."

That was news to Sam, but he wasn't surprised. It was like Carla to go the extra mile to help a troubled kid, even one who'd hurt her.

He looked at Ron and saw that he was still waiting for an answer.

"You'll have to ask her that."

"I did. She just smiled and said I'd figure it out sometime."

"Have you?"

Ron shook his head. "Not yet."

"It'll come to you."

"Jared said she was something special."

"What do you think?"

"He was right."

At dinner that evening, Carla couldn't stop talking about Ron.

At last Sam put up a hand. "Okay, okay. He's the best thing to come along since sliced bread. Now, how about paying some attention to your husband?"

She gave him a sheepish smile. "Guess I sort of got carried away."

"Just a bit."

"I'm sorry. I'm just excited for Ron. He has so much talent. All he needed was an outlet."

Sam drew her into his arms. He understood her desire to believe that Ron had changed. He only hoped she wouldn't be disappointed. He'd do anything to spare her, but he knew he couldn't shield her from all the ugliness in the world. He'd already tried that. And failed.

CHAPTER FOUR

"That's it, Sissie," Carla called. "Keep the ball moving."

Sissie dodged the girl assigned to guard her, jumping to make a basket. "I swished it," she yelled. "Nothing but net."

"Good one," Carla praised. "Okay. Who's next?"

The second girl took her turn. They went down the line until everyone had practiced the maneuver.

"We're gonna beat those Wilmont wimps next week for sure," Sissie said.

Carla tried to look stern despite the smile twitching at her lips. "What did I tell you about good sportsmanship?"

Sissie bit her lip. "Sorry."

"Okay, girls, hit the showers."

Smiling, Carla watched as the girls raced toward the locker room, giggling and shouting. Far from being tired after a two-hour practice, they had energy to spare. She had started to gather up the balls when a hesitant cough made her turn around.

"Uh, Reverend . . . Carla . . ." Ron Franks stood in front of her, holding something behind his back.

"Hi, Ron. I'm afraid you're too late to watch practice." She knew Ron liked Sissie and often came by to walk her home after practice.

Dark color smudged his cheeks. "I, uh, I didn't come for that. This is for you." He thrust a clumsily wrapped package into her hands.

"For me?"

He nodded. "It's not much. Just something I was messing around with, and I thought you might . . . Aren't you going to open it?" he asked as she continued to hold it.

She pulled at the wrapping. When the last of the paper fell away, she couldn't speak. She could only stare at the oil painting of herself.

"If you don't like it, you don't have to keep it," he said, bringing her back to reality.

"It's b-beautiful," she said, swallowing around the lump in her throat. "How . . . when . . ."

"I did some sketches when you weren't

noticing. I finished it last night. Do you like it?"

"Of course I like it. I *love* it. It's just that —"

"It's yours."

She hugged him to her. "Thank you."

He pulled away quickly. "It's okay. Uh, Carla?"

She looked up.

"About what I did . . . to the church and all . . . I feel like a real jerk. Especially since I got to know you and Sam. You're pretty cool."

She touched his shoulder. "It's in the past, Ron. Let it stay there."

"You really mean that, don't you?"

"I wouldn't say it if I didn't."

The relief that crossed his face touched her. "I'm glad you and Sam are getting along." She'd worried about that. Sam was so protective of her, she'd feared he would never give Ron a chance.

"Sam's okay," Ron allowed gruffly.

"Yeah." She smiled softly. "I think so too."

"What do you think?" Carla asked when she showed the painting to Sam that evening.

Sam studied the painting. Ron had captured Carla's essence. Compassion and love and humor shone from her eyes. Her lips were full, slightly parted, giving her a vulnerable look. "It's beautiful," he said quietly. "Just like you."

"Do I really look like that?"

He heard the doubt in her tone. "Don't you know how beautiful you are?"

"I figured Ron took a little artistic license."

"The only he thing he did was to paint you as you are." He watched as a slow flush stained her cheeks.

"The kid's got real talent," he said. "What are we going to do about it?"

"Do about it?"

"Isn't that what you had in mind?" He smiled at her sheepish expression.

"I thought we might establish some kind of scholarship fund. For kids like Ron and Jared. I know just the person to help us get started."

"Who?"

"Your mom."

Sam went silent. He was still struggling to admit his parents into his life. They'd never win any awards as parents of the year, but he was beginning to see them as decent people with their own brand of love to offer. It was up to him to find a way to accept it — and them.

He knew Carla was waiting for his response. "I think that's a great idea. If there's one thing my mother's good at, it's wrangling money from people."

The smile on Carla's face was reason enough to give a relationship with his parents a second chance.

"Good. Let's go see her."

"Now?"

"Why not?"

Sam knew when he'd been outmaneuvered.

An hour later, he listened while Carla explained her idea to his mother.

Jeanette looked surprised, then pleased at the request. "I know. We'll hold an auction. Ask everyone to contribute something and then invite them to attend. People love to think they're getting a bargain." She smiled conspiratorially. "I've got a lot of favors to call in. I've just been waiting for the right occasion."

Laughter filled the room as his mother and Carla discussed ideas. Recognizing that he wasn't needed, Sam moved to a corner desk, flipped open his laptop computer, and started drafting a proposal for the city council. The laughter came again, a soft ripple of sound that caused him to swivel in his chair, trying to figure out what his mother and his wife found so funny.

He gave up all pretense of working, his

concentration shot. As far back as he could remember, his mother had never laughed with him about anything. The realization didn't bother him as much as it intrigued him. Carla had delved beneath the surface Jeanette presented to the world and found a friend.

He listened as his mother telephoned her friends and wheedled, cajoled, and gently bullied donations from them. Within an hour, she had solicited twenty contributions, ranging from antique furniture to original oil paintings to a pedigreed puppy.

"I'll make some more calls tonight," she promised, patting Carla's hand. "Don't you worry. We'll make enough to fund the scholarships. And then some."

"Your mother's great," Carla said on the way home. "I should ask her to chair our Christmas food drive."

Sam didn't have to pretend enthusiasm for the idea this time. He'd seen the sparkle in his mother's eyes when Carla asked for her help.

Carla faced the twelve people who sat on the church advisory committee. Receiving an invitation to attend wasn't entirely a surprise. She had a feeling she knew what it was about. She also had a feeling she wasn't going to like it. The day had started miserably with an appointment at the dentist, who'd filled her tooth with entirely too much pleasure. It seemed only fitting the day should end with being called on the carpet by the people who'd hired her.

Her hands folded in her lap, she waited. After the preliminaries, the chairman opened the meeting to discussion.

Thelma Harvey sighed with long suffering patience before rising.

Carla recognized the sigh. She'd heard enough of them from Thelma in the past. Such sighs served as a prelude to the unpleasant topics the woman felt compelled to raise. Carla braced herself for what was coming.

"Reverend Hastings," Thelma began. "Is it true you hired that boy who vandalized the church last winter to do posters for the church dance?"

Carla held the older woman's gaze. "Yes, Thelma. It's true."

"How could you allow that — that animal inside our chapel? The chapel he desecrated. Have you forgotten what he did? What he wrote about you, about all of us?"

Thelma's voice shook, and for a moment Carla sympathized with her. Images of the ugly images and vicious words Ron had splashed across the walls of the church swirled through her mind. Then she pictured the pain in his eyes when he'd confessed his part in the vandalism. He needed their forgiveness, not their censure.

"Ron Franks is a fifteen-year-old boy who made a mistake. At the time he thought he didn't have any options. I want to show him he has choices" — her voice strengthened as she thought about the chance they'd been given — "and I want to show him he has friends."

"Reverend, maybe you should tell us how he came to do what he did," one of the church elders suggested.

She recounted what Jared had told her. "Ron was wrong in what he did. He knows that. Can we deny him the chance to repent?"

Murmurs of approval swept through the room. But that didn't erase the rebukes she read in the faces of Thelma and several others.

"There's one more thing we need to consider. We have the opportunity to help someone who needs our love, our forgiveness. Can we afford to reject that? And if we do" — she paused, letting her gaze meet that of everyone present — "what does that say about us?" She waited for her words to sink in. "Ron did what he felt he had to do for his family to survive. I can't condone his actions, but I can understand why."

Thelma gave an audible sniff as she sat down. "If you believe in him so much, why haven't you had him in your home?"

"He's visited my house twice in the last week," Carla said quietly. "I've also invited him to services next Sunday. I'm hoping he'll attend."

The murmurs she heard this time were hardly encouraging, but she pressed on. "We have a chance to help a boy find a new way to live. I can't turn my back on that." She felt Thelma's gaze on her and deliberately let her eyes meet the older woman's. "Can you?"

"I say we trust the reverend on this," the chairman said before Thelma had a chance to answer. "She believes in the boy. That's good enough for me."

"Well, it's not for me." Thelma stood once more, smoothed her skirt, and walked out. Several others followed her.

Carla drew a shaky breath. She looked around at the people whom she'd promised to serve. They were good people, honest and sincere in their beliefs. They deserved her best. So did Ron.

Some squeezed her hand as they filed

past. Others smiled and gave her a thumbs-up.

Mrs. Miller patted her shoulder. "Stick to your guns, dear. You do what you have to do to help that boy. We're behind you."

"Thank you," Carla said. "I wish everyone felt the same way you do."

"Thelma will come around," Mrs. Miller predicted. "She's lonely. Sometimes that makes people say things they don't really mean." She gave a rueful smile. "I know I'm just a silly old woman who gossips too much. But I hear things. And I know Thelma thinks the world of you. When you helped her look for Grover Cleveland, well, she broke down telling me about it. It meant everything to her."

Carla smiled at this woman whose heart was as big as her girth. Mrs. Miller had looked past Thelma's pettiness and seen the loneliness behind it. Why hadn't she been able to do the same?

She asked Sam that very question over dinner that evening.

"You're doing it again," he said.

"Doing what?"

"Being too hard on yourself."

She thought about it. Maybe Sam was right. She leaned over to kiss him. "How did you get so smart?"

"Easy. I had a good teacher."

"So what am I supposed to do about Thelma and the rest? Do I have the right to ask Ron to church knowing how they feel about him?"

"Only you can answer that," was Sam's reply.

The question plagued her far into the night. Could she ask her congregation to accept Ron after what he'd done? Did she have the right? Suddenly she smiled. She needed help. And she knew just where to find it.

The next morning, Carla told Ethan and Maude Sandberg about Ron. The elderly couple had supported Carla in the past; they reacted as she'd predicted.

"What can we do to help?" Maude asked.

Carla smiled at her no-nonsense approach. No reproach, no recrimination, just an offer to help. That was Ethan and Maude. Practicality mixed with a generous dose of compassion.

"It doesn't matter to you what he did?" she asked. She had to make sure.

Ethan scratched his head. "That boy did something mighty bad, but it sounds like he's trying to make up for it. Can't rightly hold that against him."

If only everyone shared the same feeling.

The following day she brought Ron by to meet them.

Ethan stuck out his hand. "Glad to meet you, young fellow."

Maude bustled out of the kitchen, wiping her hands on an old-fashioned bib apron. "I just pulled a pan of cookies out of the oven."

"Chocolate chip?" Ron asked.

"Is there any other kind?" Maude chuckled. "Come on. They're best when they're hot."

Ethan winked at Ron. "Best do what she says. She wields a mean spatula when she's riled." He followed his wife into the kitchen.

Ron threw a helpless look at Carla. "Are they for real?"

She smothered a smile.

He put away half a dozen cookies, washing them down with a couple of glasses of milk. He wiped his mouth on his sleeve, looked up, and smiled sheepishly.

Samson jumped on him, licking his face.

"Looks like it's love at first sight," Ethan said. "You sure you don't mind having that silly mutt slobber all over you?"

"I don't mind," the boy said. "All right with you if I take him for a walk?"

"Sure." Ethan attached the leash to Samson's collar and handed it to Ron.

"Mind he doesn't get away from you," Maude said. "He's as frisky as some people I know on the first day of spring." She gave her husband a fond look.

Ethan's chest puffed out. "Frisky, is it? I kinda like that. Makes me sound like —"

"Ethan." He trailed off at the soft rebuke in Maude's voice.

Carla chuckled. She spent the next hour visiting with them until Ron returned. If he came to church on Sunday, she was satisfied he'd have at least two friends.

On Sunday morning, she scanned the congregation and bit her lip in disappointment when she didn't see Ron. Well, she'd known it was unlikely that he'd accept her invitation. Still, she'd hoped. . . .

Suddenly there was a commotion at the rear of the church, and she leaned forward across the pulpit. Murmurs rippled through the chapel, and she knew Ron was there even before she saw him. He hesitated before sliding into the pew occupied by Ethan and Maude. She smiled as she saw Ethan grip Ron's hand. It was going to be all right.

Still, she couldn't completely quell her misgivings as she saw the stares some of the members of the congregation directed at him. The glances ranged from open curiosity to compassion to antagonism. Ron returned the looks with a steady gaze, and her heart swelled with pride for him.

Her sermon centered on the theme of forgiveness. When her voice broke at one point, she sought Sam's gaze. What she saw in his eyes gave her the strength to continue. His quiet presence had sustained her more than once during a difficult Sunday service. She smiled at him tremulously.

By the end of her sermon, she'd relaxed enough to sing the closing hymn with her usual enthusiasm. Following the benediction, she made her way to the rear of the chapel, where she shook hands with the congregation as they filed out.

Thelma Harvey paused before holding out her hand. "An interesting sermon today, Reverend."

Carla pressed the veined hand. "Thank you, Thelma. It's good to see you here."

"Good sermon, Reverend," Mrs. Miller said, straightening her flowered hat. "Wasn't it, young man?" she asked, turning to Ron.

"Uh, yes."

"Good to have you here. Come visit sometime. The reverend will give you the address." Jamming her hat more firmly on her head, she sailed past them.

Ron look bemused.

Carla understood. Mrs. Miller frequently had the same effect on her. "I'm glad you came."

"So am I." He looked surprised. "I got a job. Maude and Ethan asked me to walk Samson after school each day."

"That's great." She had long ago stopped trying to keep the Sandbergs from spending their meager pension helping others. She could hardly criticize them for doing as she preached.

He glanced at the line of people waiting to talk with her. "I'll see you later."

"You did it," Sam said, slipping his arms around her waist when they were alone.

She leaned against him. "It wasn't me. It was Maude and Ethan and Mrs. Miller and —"

He turned her in his arms and silenced her by pressing a kiss to her lips. He'd never convince her that it was her magic that sparked love in others.

Still basking in the warmth she had felt the day before at church, Carla was unprepared for the call.

"Carla, it's Maude. Samson's gone."

Carla gripped the receiver to her. "I'll be there in five minutes."

Sam let himself in just as she was preparing to leave.

"Samson's missing."

He called the police before they left for the Sandbergs' house. She listened as he explained the situation.

"They'll meet us there," he said upon hanging up.

A black-and-white squad car was already parked in front of the Sandbergs' house when they arrived.

Carla offered to answer whatever questions the police might have. Ethan gave her a grateful look and took Maude to the bedroom.

"You say he's a Scottie." The officer pulled out a notebook and jotted something down.

"Mostly."

His lips quirked. "Mostly?"

But Carla was in no mood to appreciate the joke. "He's black with white around the face. He answers to the name of Samson."

The officer raised his eyebrows. "Samson?"

"You know, from the Bible."

"Uh huh." He turned his attention to Sam. "Anything you can tell us, Mr. Hastings?"

"Only what we told you the last time. This isn't an ordinary dognapping. None of these people have money to pay a ransom. There's something else going on."

"Why don't we let the detectives determine that?"

The police continued their questioning, but Carla and Sam could only add a little to what they'd already told them. The officers were efficient and polite. They were also discouraging about the chances of finding the stolen pets.

"The Sandbergs are really upset about Samson," Carla said. "Do you have any idea when you might —"

"It's like this, Reverend," the older policeman said. "We get a dozen calls every night. Throw in the occasional robbery or mugging and we've got more than we can handle. Finding a missing dog . . ." He shrugged. "A couple of detectives will probably be assigned to the case, but I wouldn't expect too much."

Carla nodded. She appreciated his honesty, but it didn't help her explain to Maude and Ethan that they might never see Samson again. "Thank you for coming."

The officer touched his hat and was turning to leave when Sam stopped him. "You'll let us know if you learn anything?"

"Of course, sir."

Carla and Sam spent the rest of the

evening trying to cheer up Maude and Ethan, but she knew their efforts fell flat. When the older couple valiantly tried to hide yawns, she and Sam took their leave.

Carla was quiet on the way home. Too quiet, Sam thought, slanting her a worried look. He knew her well enough to guess what she was thinking. He also knew he wasn't going to like it.

"They're not going to do anything," Carla said.

"They'll file a report. Some detectives will ask a few questions, and —"

"That will be the end of it."

"I'm afraid so."

"Then it's up to us."

The determined set of her chin and the look in her eyes warned him what was coming. Trying to keep Carla out of a mystery was like trying to keep a small boy from licking a bowl of cake batter. Still, he felt compelled to try to dissuade her. "Maybe we're selling the police short. They're —"

"Swamped with other cases. More important cases," she finished for him.

He couldn't argue with that.

Her eyes glinted with excitement. "We can do it. I know we can. Didn't we solve the warehouse mystery?"

He shuddered at the memories of Carla in

the hands of the coldly calculating woman who'd kidnapped her. "And you nearly got killed." He never wanted to live through a time like that again.

"But I didn't." She gave him a pleading look. "We have to do something, Sam. First Thelma's Grover Cleveland, then the Millers' Collette, and now Samson. Those dogs are members of the family."

With a groan, Sam pulled her to him, burying his head in her hair. He inhaled the scent of her shampoo, something citrusy and fresh, and sighed. He knew when he was beaten. He'd known it before they started the conversation. "We'll look into it — on one condition."

She pushed away slightly to look up at him suspiciously. "What's that?"

"We do it my way. That means no going off on your own. No taking chances. No —"

"Sam, I'm a grown woman. I know how to take care of myself. I've been doing it for a long time."

"I know," he said, taking her hand in his. It was small but had an underlying strength. Like Carla herself. "Humor me, okay?"

Her brow furrowed into a frown. "You think there's more going on than three missing dogs?"

"I don't know. But I'm not taking any

chances. Not with you." He raised their linked hands and brushed his lips over her knuckles. "We do it together."

"You're cute when you're being overprotective."

"If anything happened to you . . ." He couldn't complete the thought, even to himself.

"Nothing will happen to me. I'm just going to ask a few questions, put out some feelers on the street."

Sam knew Carla considered the street people her friends. For the most part, they were. He also knew that she was vulnerable on the streets because of that belief. Loving Carla meant giving her the freedom to do what she felt she had to. Loving her also meant keeping her safe. It was a dilemma he had yet to solve.

"It's settled then," she said, smiling.

It was far from settled as far as Sam was concerned.

George wandered in, saving him from saying something he'd probably regret.

"Hear that, boy?" Carla asked, scratching the dog behind the ears. "Sam and I are going to find Samson. You don't have to be sad anymore."

Sam knew better than to ask, but he couldn't help himself. "Why is George sad?"

"Because Samson's missing."

"Carla, George can't be sad because Samson's missing."

"Why not?"

"Because . . ." Sam raked his fingers through his hair. "Because he's a dog."

"So?"

"So, dogs can't be sad because another dog is missing. He doesn't even know Samson that well." Realizing what he'd just said, Sam winced. He was discussing a dog's emotional state with every appearance of seriousness. He shook his head, wondering what this said about his sanity, then decided he didn't really want to know.

"George is very sensitive," she said. "He understands more than we realize."

George woofed.

Thomas backed him up with a shrill meow.

Carla gave Sam a triumphant smile. "See?"

The following day Carla headed home, more discouraged than she wanted to admit. Three hours on the street asking questions and receiving nothing but negative answers had made her doubt there was anything to learn.

As she walked home along a busy street,

she suddenly saw a boy slice a knife through an elderly woman's purse strap, yanking it from her arm. Carla reacted automatically and chased after him. The boy wove in and out between the people on the sidewalk. When he saw Carla didn't intend to give up the chase, he threw the purse to the side and ducked down an alley.

She retrieved the purse and ran back to the woman.

"Thank you, dear," the older woman said when Carla handed the purse to her. "I don't know what I'd have done if I had lost my purse. My dog's been missing for three days. I'm on my way to put an ad in the newspaper right now." She opened her purse. "Let me give you something for your trouble."

Carla shook her head. "You don't owe me a thing. But I was wondering, do you have time for a cup of coffee?"

Twenty minutes later, she was sitting in a booth in a doughnut shop across from the woman, who had introduced herself as Ethel Hillman.

"Tell me about your dog," Carla invited after they'd ordered.

"Charlie's a toy poodle. He's four years old. One evening, I let him out, and he just didn't come in. He was gone."

"I supposed you checked the neighbor-hood."

"Several times over. After the first day I put up posters, offering a reward. If I don't find him . . ." Ethel's voice broke. She shook her head. "I'm sorry. It's silly to get so upset over a dog. But he's all I have."

Carla took the other woman's hand in her own. "It's not silly. You love Charlie."

Ethel gave her a grateful look. "You do understand, don't you?"

"Yes," Carla said softly. "I do." She pulled a pen from her purse and scribbled her name and phone number on a napkin. "Will you let me know if — when — you find Charlie?"

Their eyes met in silent understanding.

Ethel folded the napkin and put it in her purse. "Thank you for listening to an old woman."

"That makes four that we know of," Carla said, repeating the conversation to Sam when she returned home.

"Maybe a lot more than that."

"And we're no closer to finding out what's going on than we were two weeks ago. What are we going to do?"

"I don't know," he admitted. He covered

her hand with his. "We'll find them. I promise."

Three hours later, as he waited for Carla to dress for the church dance, he wondered if he could make good on his promise. She was right. They were no nearer to discovering what had happened to the dogs than they had been weeks ago. He had a feeling that things were going to get worse before they got better.

He yawned, regretting he'd agreed to chaperone the dance tonight. He looked longingly at the sofa, where George laying snoring. "How 'bout trading places tonight, boy?"

All thoughts of missing dogs vanished from his mind when Carla appeared. She wore a deep blue dress, her hair falling in soft curls around her face. His breath caught in his throat before shuddering to a sigh. Chaperoning a kids' dance suddenly looked pretty good, he decided, crossing the room to take her in his arms. More than good, he thought a few moments later as he fitted his lips to hers.

The spinning glass ball scattered tiny prisms of light across the church recreation hall. Cardboard palm trees, baskets of papier-mâché fruit, and crepe paper flowers had

transformed the room into a tropical para-
dise.

"Looks like Ron's posters did the trick,"
Carla said, gesturing to the packed room.

Sam looked at the twisting, gyrating bod-
ies around him and wondered how he'd
manage to become one of them. The answer
wasn't hard to find.

Carla.

He hadn't danced like this since he was a
kid. What's more, he was enjoying it. Or he
would as soon as he caught his breath.

"Time out," he said, leading her from the
floor. He headed to the refreshment table.
Even sugary red punch sounded good right
now. He'd forgotten that dancing was such
hard work.

"You weren't bad out there," she said.

"For an old guy?" He picked up a paper
cup of punch, grimacing as he washed it
down with a cookie. Cookies and punch.
He felt as if he'd been transported by a time
machine back to the days of dancing les-
sons and the mandatory cotillions that his
dance teacher felt compelled to hold every
month.

She laughed, a soft ripple of sound, and
he joined in.

"Tell me again how come we're here

instead of at home curled up in bed and —"

She put a finger to her lips. "Shh. Somebody will hear you."

His laugh erupted into a full-fledged guffaw. "Carla, nobody's going to hear anything. Not with this racket."

"How can you call the latest rock music racket?"

"Easy. I've got excellent hearing." He tugged at his ear. "Or at least I used to."

"Come on," she said, grabbing his hand. "Let's show 'em how it's done."

He followed her onto the dance floor, grateful when the band changed to a slow love song, and drew her into his arms. She slipped her arms around his neck. Together they swayed gently in time to the music.

". . . love's sweet promise is all I have to give," the lead singer crooned.

Instinctively Sam tightened his arms around Carla. There was something to be said about dances after all, he decided, savoring the way she melted against him. They danced through four more songs, each one more romantic than the last. Or maybe he was feeling more romantic with every passing moment. He felt himself responding to the tug of the mellow lyrics.

"You were saying something about being

too old for this?" Carla teased softly, her breath fanning his cheek.

"I just got my second wind."

They continued dancing, oblivious to their surroundings, until someone tapped him on the shoulder.

"Hey, Mr. Hastings, the music's stopped."

Sam looked around. Everyone else had stopped dancing and had gathered around them. A couple of boys snickered while the girls giggled.

"Guess you didn't notice, huh?" a boy asked.

"Guess I didn't." Sam glanced at Carla, wondering if she was embarrassed.

Her eyes held no trace of embarrassment, only amusement.

"Let's give 'em a real show," he whispered. He kissed her on the lips. The kiss, which he'd intended to keep light and easy, lingered and deepened until he forgot about the crowd of kids surrounding them, forgot he was in the church recreation hall, forgot everything but the woman in his arms. Startled into awareness by a round of applause, he looked up, dazed. He should have known better. Kissing Carla had short-circuited his brain.

"You're all right, Mr. Hastings," a girl with bright pink hair said.

"Yeah," her date seconded. "The chaperones we usually have never kiss." The boy gave an admiring whistle. "At least not like that."

Sam grinned ruefully. "Guess I just ruined our reputation."

Carla laughed. "I'd say you just made it."

She was still smiling when they returned home, singing lyrics from old love songs. She twirled around the floor, taking Sam with her.

". . . love's sweet promise . . ."

The shrill ring of the phone interrupted them. She reached to answer it.

"Reverend Hastings?" an unfamiliar voice asked.

"Yes?"

"You look like a smart lady. You wanna stay that way, you keep your nose clean."

The words were muffled, as though they came from inside a tunnel, and she strained to make them out. "I don't —"

"Don't go sniffing around after those dogs." The caller sniggered, obviously pleased at his joke. "Not if you know what's good for you." The voice was vaguely familiar, but she couldn't place it. The caller was obviously trying to disguise it.

She stared at the receiver for several moments before registering the buzz of the dial tone. Slowly she recradled the phone.

Sam gathered her to him. "What is it?"

She repeated the terse warning, trembling even as his arms closed around her.

CHAPTER FIVE

Last night's call still lodged in his mind, Sam hovered as Carla prepared to visit two members of her congregation in the hospital.

"You sure you don't want me to go with you?" he asked. "I could carry the flowers."

"I'm sure I don't want you worrying about me," she said, standing on tiptoe to kiss him. "But I love you for it." She flashed him a smile that never failed to elicit one from him. "Besides, I don't have any flowers."

"We could go get some together."

"Sam, Mrs. Lindquist is allergic to flowers, remember? And old Mr. Donaldson would rather have these." She pointed to a pile of magazines.

He sighed. She'd seen right through him. He resisted the urge to order her to stay home today. He knew what kind of reaction *that* was likely to receive.

She placed her palm on his cheek. "I'll be

fine. People who make anonymous threats are cowards at heart."

"You can't be sure about that."

"No. But I can't live my life being afraid of my own shadow because some creep decides to play games on the phone." She gave him a steady look. "What would you do if you had gotten the call? Ignore it, right?"

He thought about denying it and knew he couldn't. Carla knew him too well. "That's different."

"It's exactly the same. And you know it."

She had him there. "You win."

The smile she gave him was as mischievous as the spark in her eyes. "Good."

After extracting a promise from her to be careful, he saw her off and then picked up the phone. It was time he made some inquiries of his own.

An hour later, he glanced impatiently out his rearview mirror. The traffic snarl he was caught in gave no appearance of unraveling any time soon. He settled back in the seat to wait. And worry.

He'd never convince Carla to drop the investigation. After her initial fear, which had been quickly supplanted by anger, she'd been more determined than ever to pursue it. Whoever thought they could scare her off with threats had underestimated her. That left him with a big problem. He had to keep Carla safe. And that meant he had to find the dogs. Soon.

A horn blared and he pressed on the accelerator. "Okay, okay," he muttered.

Outside the city limits, he picked up speed. He'd done some checking with the bureau of records and had learned the name and address of a medical research lab. Located approximately twenty miles from the city, it sat by itself in a field.

He drove slowly now, wanting to get a feel for the place. A chain link fence discouraged trespassers. No landscaping softened the concrete structure. The building itself was nondescript, squat, and gray. The only sign was small, with discreet lettering identifying it as Cobe Laboratories for the Advancement of Medical Research.

He pulled into one of the few parking spaces. Inside the lobby, he gave his name to the security guard.

"What's your business?"

"I'm investigating some stolen pets."

The guard, who looked more like a bouncer in a downtown club, rolled impressive-looking shoulders. "So investigate. Somewhere else."

"Look, all I want to do is ask some questions."

"I told you, we don't know nothing."

"Maybe if I could talk to someone in charge . . ."

A slender, graying man appeared at that moment. "Howard Garrity," he introduced himself. "What seems to be the problem here?"

Sam told Garrity his name and found his hand caught in a surprisingly strong grip.

"Glad to meet you, Councilman Hastings." Garrity turned his attention to the guard. "Dax, I'll take it from here."

The guard gave Sam a long look before resuming his place at the door.

"Why don't we step into my office?" Garrity suggested.

The office was as nondescript as the exterior of the building. Spartan furnishings didn't invite visitors to linger. Sam settled into a hard-backed chair.

"I'm sorry about what happened out there," Garrity said, gesturing to the lobby. "Dax tends to take his duties a little too seriously at times. Understandable, of course, since we deal with some confidential material. Now what can I do for you?"

Sam repeated his story, watching the other man carefully for any telltale reaction.

Garrity's expression remained bland as he spread his hands in a gesture of regret. "I'm sorry I can't help you. We buy our animals from reputable dealers."

"Perhaps if I could see some of the dogs you have here —"

"I wish I could help you, but our facilities are private. I'm sure you understand." He stood. "If you'll forgive the pun, I'm afraid you're barking up the wrong tree."

Sam forced a smile. "Thank you for your time."

"You're most welcome. Now if you'll excuse me . . ."

Sam took the hint and stood. In the lobby he met a smiling Dax.

"You finish your investigation?" the guard asked.

"Not yet."

"Too bad." Dax held the door open with obvious pleasure.

Sam's visit had netted him a big fat zero. He was no closer to finding the dogs or to discovering who had made the threat against Carla. All he could do was stick as close as possible to her.

And pray it would be enough.

"Here you go," Carla said, placing a cup of

juice and a sandwich in a child's chubby hands.

"Thank you, ma'am."

She bent to kiss the child's cheek. "You're welcome."

The warmer weather eased the need on the streets but didn't erase it. Blankets and coats were no longer in demand, but food was. Hunger knew no season. She and Sam distributed food twice a week. With increased funds from the city council, they were able to provide meals for more than a hundred people.

Standing on the curb, she felt something shove her between the shoulder blades. She floundered, trying to catch her balance as she fell on her hands and knees in the middle of the street. She heard a rumbling noise and looked up. A pickup truck barreled toward her. It was close enough that she smelled the exhaust of the engine as the fumes swirled around her, felt the spray of gravel it kicked up sting her face.

Move, her brain screamed.

A running force shoved her out of the way. She hit the ground — hard — then rolled to the side of the street. She heard the roar of the truck as it streaked by.

Stunned, she lay where she'd landed, her breath coming in sharp pants, her skin cold and clammy despite the warmth of the night.

"Carla?"

The voice — was it Sam's? — seemed to come from far away. She lifted her gaze. Sam's face blurred before sharpening into focus.

"Carla?" He ran his hands over her. "Are you all right?" Gentle hands helped her to her feet, a contrast to the rough urgency in his voice.

Still trembling, she huddled in his arms. "I think so." She looked up at his face, gray in the muted light from the street lamps. His hands shook, and only then did she realize how close she'd come to being killed.

She started to take his hands in hers and stopped, staring. His shirt was torn, the ripped fabric revealing a gash down his arm. The sight of his blood jolted her out of her shock. "You're bleeding."

He looked down. "It's just a scratch."

"Scratch nothing." She helped him remove his shirt. The "scratch" ran several inches long with blood oozing from it. For a moment, the world spun. She bit down on her lip. The pain steadied her.

"You sure you're all right?" he asked.

"I'm sure." She wrapped a towel around his arm. "We're going to the hospital."

"We're going home."

"Sam Hastings, I'm not arguing with you when you're bleeding."

"Good. Because I don't feel like arguing."

Twenty minutes later, he was sitting in a cubicle of the emergency room while a doctor stitched up his arm.

"You were lucky," the doctor said when Sam gave an abbreviated account of what had happened.

The doctor was right. He *was* lucky. But not for the reason the doctor gave. Sam looked at Carla and gave a silent prayer of thanks that she was all right. If he'd been a fraction of a second slower . . . A shudder rippled through him as he pictured Carla, broken and smashed beneath the truck's tires.

"Yeah. Lucky."

The doctor handed Carla a bottle of pills. "He'll need these as soon as that shot I gave him wears off. Come morning, he's going to feel like a truck ran over him." He chuckled at his joke.

"I don't need —"

She dropped the pills in her purse. "I'll see that he takes them."

Sam must have dozed on the way home, for soon Carla was gently shaking him awake. "Sam. We're home."

With her help, he made it to the house and into their bedroom. His arm was throbbing.

"Here," she said, handing him a pill and a glass of water.

"No." The word came out as a grunt as a spasm of pain crawled down his arm.

She simply waited.

"Okay, okay," he muttered. He swallowed the painkiller. Within minutes he could feel its numbing effects. But he had to stay awake long enough to tell Carla something.

"The truck —"

"It can wait till morning."

"It wasn't an accident."

"I know." He saw the acknowledgement in her eyes. "I wanted to believe it was. But I saw the driver's eyes. He meant to . . ." Her words shivered to a stop.

He reached for her hand. "I should never have let you go out." The bitter taste of guilt tainted his mouth. He'd promised to protect her, and he'd failed.

"You saved my life. Now I'm going to take care of you."

She settled him in bed. He tucked her beside him, her sweet warmth more quieting than any pill.

Hours later, the nightmare swam through his mind. Carla . . . the truck. He jerked awake. The sheets smelled of sweat and fear. He could have lost Carla.

Tomorrow he'd tell her that it was over. No more investigating. No more asking questions. Whatever objections she made, he'd override. He felt her stir beside him. The soft sigh she gave when he pulled her to him caused him to tighten his arm around her. She made a tiny sound of protest, and he loosened his hold. She turned on her side and nestled against him.

He let the rhythm of her breathing lull him to sleep.

When he awoke, Carla was gone. He jerked up, only to grunt and lie back as his body registered a complaint. He ached all over.

He inhaled the aroma of bacon and eggs appreciatively. When Carla came in bearing a tray of food, he sat up cautiously.

"How are you feeling?" she asked, setting the tray on the nightstand.

"How do I look?"

"Terrible."

"Thanks."

She handed him a glass of juice and a pill.

"I don't want —"

"Too bad. You're going to take it."

"Anybody ever tell you that you have a lousy bedside manner?"

She bent to kiss his forehead. "Only the lousy patients." She tapped his hand. "Come on. Bottoms up." She stood over him until he swallowed the pill, washing it down with orange juice.

"Satisfied?"

"I will be as soon as you eat your breakfast."

"Are you joining me?"

She looked flustered. "Uh, no. I've already eaten."

She was up to something. He was sure of it. He was also pretty sure he knew what it was. "Spill it."

"What?"

"Whatever it is you're up to."

"Who says I'm up to anything?" Her eyes were wide with innocence.

"I do."

"You've got a suspicious mind, Sam Hastings."

"I plead guilty as charged." He folded his arms across his chest, waiting.

Still, she said nothing.

"You're planning on hitting the streets." Her sigh confirmed his guess. "After what happened last night?"

"That was at night," she said. "No one's going to try anything in broad daylight."

"You don't know that. Last night proves

someone's getting pretty desperate."

"I won't go anywhere dangerous," she promised. "Just down to Central Park to ask some questions."

It wasn't a bad idea. People living on the streets frequently knew what was going on more than the police. But there was no way he would let her go alone.

He pushed the tray aside and started to get up, biting back a groan as his battered muscles protested.

Gently she pushed him back in bed. That she could handle him with so little effort forced him to realize just how sore he still was.

"You're in no condition to go anywhere," she said.

"You're not going alone."

In the end, they compromised. Sam agreed to spend the morning in bed, after extracting a promise from her that she'd stay home and work on her sermon. Then they'd go out in the afternoon and start asking questions.

Carla knew what Sam was doing. Suggesting they start at the shelter was his way of keeping her safe. But she couldn't object. Visiting Saratoga's shelter for the homeless was something she never tired of.

Today it hummed with activity: A basketball game occupied the recreation hall, where a makeshift court had been set up; an adult education class was being held in the office; an aerobics group worked out in the dining area.

Her smile grew as she saw Jared patiently instruct a small child on the right way to dribble. He had volunteered to coach a peewee basketball team made up of kids currently staying at the shelter. When he saw Sam and Carla, he said something to the younger boys and headed over to them.

"Hey, guys. You come down to get in some practice? Maybe improve your jump shot?" He slanted a smile at Sam. "How 'bout a game of one on one?"

"You looking for a chance to show off in front of the kids?"

"Just 'cause I beat you the last five games doesn't mean I'd win this one."

"Thanks."

"Okay, you two," Carla said. "Enough of this male macho stuff." She leaned forward to kiss Jared on the cheek, smiling as he looked around furtively to see if any of the kids had noticed.

Apparently satisfied, he grinned. "What brings you two here?"

"Questions," she said. "About the dogs."

"You hear anything down here?" Sam asked.

Jared shook his head. "I wish I had. You know how I feel about Maude and Ethan. If I ever find out who took Samson . . ." His hands fisted on his hips.

Sam looped an arm around the boy's shoulders.

"Yeah. I know. Just keep your eyes and ears open, okay?"

"You got it."

After talking to a few more of the shelter's residents, they stopped again to say good-bye to Jared.

"Seen Ron around?" Sam asked.

Jared frowned. "Not lately. Why?"

"No reason," she said quickly, flashing a warning look at Sam.

They spent the rest of the afternoon asking questions on the street, with the same result. No one knew anything. Or, if they did, they weren't talking.

"C'mon," Sam said, tugging at her hand as the sky darkened. "You're dead on your feet." He gave her a strained smile. "And so am I."

She looked at him in quick concern. His face was drawn and pinched. *My fault,* she berated herself. She'd been so anxious to find some clue to the dogs' disappearance that she'd forgotten Sam was still recovering.

At home, she made sure Sam took a painkiller before bullying him into bed.

When the doorbell rang, she hurried to answer it, not wanting to disturb Sam.

Jared stood there.

"Can't stay away from us?" she asked, gesturing for him to come inside.

The smile she'd expected to see didn't materialize.

He followed her into the kitchen and accepted the soft drink she offered with a muttered thanks. He bunched his ever-present hat into his hands. "I know you think it was Stick — Ron — who snatched the dogs. But you're wrong. He wouldn't do nothing like that. It's just those old biddies trying to pin it on him. They think because a guy's messed up once, he's always trouble."

"Anything," Carla corrected automatically.

"What?"

"He wouldn't do anything."

Jared grinned. "See. You know it too."

She felt a smile tugging at her lips. She couldn't argue with Jared when he was only defending his friend. She didn't want to believe that Ron was behind the pet kidnappings, but neither could she afford to stick her head in the sand and ignore the possibility that he could be involved.

Her smile died as she realized how much she'd grown to like Ron. Rough edges and all. He was a street-smart kid who'd had more than his share of tough breaks. She thought he'd turned himself around, but maybe she'd expected too much too soon. No, she couldn't be so wrong. Ron was genuinely excited to have a job. He hadn't been faking his delight when she'd handed him the money for the posters.

"Ron's done some stupid things in the past," Jared said. "But not this. You've seen him with Samson. He loves him. And George too. He wouldn't hurt an animal."

As if on cue, George wandered in, looking from Jared to Carla. He put his paws on Jared's knees.

"You like Ron, don't you, boy?" Jared asked, letting the dog lick his face.

George woofed.

"See?" Jared demanded. "George knows Ron wouldn't do anything wrong."

"Who wouldn't do anything wrong?" Sam asked, walking into the kitchen.

"You're supposed to be sleeping," she said.

He ignored that. "Who wouldn't do what?"

Jared and Carla traded glances.

"Ron," she said reluctantly.

"Ron didn't take Samson," Jared said.

Sam looked at the boy who had so quickly become part of his life. In many ways, Jared was much like Carla, wanting to believe the best of everyone. Sam hated to see that innocence destroyed. That would happen soon enough. He had no desire to rush the process.

"I think you're right," he agreed.

Jared looked at Sam with undisguised hero worship. "I was on my way to visit Maude and Ethan. Try to cheer them up."

"Thanks, Jared," Carla said. "I just talked to them. I know they'd like to see you."

"How are they taking it?" Sam asked when Jared left.

"As you'd expect. They're trying to keep their hopes up, but I know they're hurting." She balled her hands into fists. "Who would do something like that? Take an old couple's dog."

The same kind of person who'd vandalize a church. But Sam kept the thought to himself. There was no real evidence to connect Ron to the dogs' disappearances. And Sam's instincts told him the boy was innocent.

But if not Ron, then who?

CHAPTER SIX

He knew.

One look at Ron's face and Carla knew he'd heard the rumors people were spreading about him. Carla tried to neutralize her expression, but she sensed she'd failed miserably. Her heart turned over at the look in his eyes.

"Ron . . ."

"You think I stole Samson, right?"

She heard the defensiveness in his tone, read it in his stiffening posture.

"We didn't say that —"

"Where do you get off saying I stole some dog?"

"No one believes that," Carla said, shooting Sam a pleading look. "We just wanted to know if you noticed anything when you were walking him. Maybe someone who was watching you. Anything out of the ordinary."

"I didn't see nothing."

The belligerence in the boy's voice made

her bite her lip. The last thing she wanted was to alienate Ron. He'd come so far. He needed to know someone believed in him.

What would she do if she was wrong and he *was* guilty? She pushed away the idea.

"Do you believe me?" He pinned her with his gaze.

She heard the pride in his voice. And the youthful dignity. Could he be faking? She didn't think so. "I believe you," she said quietly.

"How 'bout you?" the boy demanded of Sam, his lip curled. "You just willing to take my word on it?" The sneer didn't quite come off.

"If you say you didn't take the dog, I believe you."

"You do?" Ron's voice was hesitant this time, his eyes wary.

"Yeah. I do."

Carla poked him lightly on the arm. "C'mon. I made some brownies. With chocolate chips."

"Brownies?"

The tense moment had passed, but she knew from the wary way Ron looked from her to Sam that he didn't fully trust them.

"I believe him," Carla told Sam later.

"I know."

She wrapped her arms around him and

rested her head on his shoulder. She allowed herself the luxury of remaining there for several long moments, drawing on his strength.

When she pulled away at last, she gave him a watery smile. "You think I'm wrong."

"No. I think you're right."

She looked up in surprise. "Why?"

"You saw something decent in Ron. You know something?"

"What?"

"I saw it too."

"What if —" She didn't complete the thought.

"What if we're wrong?"

She nodded.

"It means we're human."

The atmosphere was strained. She felt it even before she took her seat. She heard the whispers, saw the raised eyebrows. She couldn't blame the members of the church advisory committee for their skepticism. Still, she kept her head up.

She didn't believe Ron was responsible for taking the dogs, but she couldn't expect everyone to share her conviction. They didn't know him as she did. They didn't understand how much he'd changed in the last few weeks.

"Well, Reverend Hastings, what do you have to say for yourself?" Thelma Harvey demanded. "You foisted that boy on us, and now look what's happened." A pinched expression around her mouth made her look even more sour than ever.

Carla took her time in answering. "I didn't *foist* Ron on anyone, Thelma. As far as the missing dogs go, we don't have any evidence that he took them."

She let her gaze sweep over the others in the room. The hostility was almost palpable. The people who had supported her last time now carefully avoided her eyes.

"Two of the dogs were missing before Ron started working on the posters," she pointed out.

"He was probably casing the joint before he actually came around," Thelma said.

Carla choked back a strangled laugh. It wasn't funny. But hearing Thelma talk like a detective from a B movie tempted her to forget that.

"Ron's a friend. I don't turn my back on my friends."

Thelma flushed.

Carla looked straight at the older woman. "Now, if you'll excuse me, I have a sermon to write." She stood and headed to the door.

"If you won't do something about it, don't

be surprised when someone else does," Thelma called after her.

Carla's footsteps faltered for a moment, but she didn't stop.

The incident left a sour taste in her mouth. She'd barely stepped inside the house when the phone rang. Sighing, she went to answer it.

"Mrs. Hastings?"

"Yes?"

"Sergeant Nichols. I spoke to your husband a couple of days ago about some missing dogs. I thought I'd better call you."

"Not another stolen dog?"

"No." Before she could even register relief, he continued. "We got a tip and brought someone in for questioning."

"Great. Did he tell you where the dogs are?"

"He denies having anything to do with it. But he'll change his tune pretty soon. Punks like him usually do after they spend a night or two in juvenile hall."

"What's his name?"

"Some kid." The rustle of paper crackled over the phone. "Name of Ron Franks."

A slow hiss escaped her lips. "That can't be right."

"Just what makes you say that?"

"I know Ron. He wouldn't steal a dog."

"The kid's been in and out of trouble for the last six months."

"Been," Carla stressed. "He's changed."

"Begging your pardon, ma'am, but a kid with that kind of record doesn't change. Leastways not without someone giving him a good old-fashioned push in the right direction."

She held on to her temper with an effort. "What evidence do you have against Ron?"

"He had access to one of the dogs. He needed the money. He's got a record."

"What about the other dogs? They were stolen weeks ago. Ron's only been coming around for the last week or so."

"That's why we're asking him about the last dog that was snatched. What was his name? Samuel — Sampini? It'll come to me."

"Samson," she said. "From the Bible."

"Yeah. Samson."

"Sergeant?"

"Yes, ma'am?"

"You're making a mistake."

"It wouldn't be the first time. In the meantime we've got a suspect. If you'll pardon me for saying so, ma'am, you and your husband have been giving the boys at the station plenty of grief over a bunch of dogs. Now that we've brought someone in, you start complaining that we've got the wrong guy. That don't sit too well with me."

She recognized she'd made a tactical error. Still, she couldn't stand by and let Ron be accused of something she knew he didn't do.

"When can I see him?"

"Anytime you want to come down." The sergeant hung up without saying good-bye.

She could hardly blame him for the abrupt way he'd ended the conversation. She'd been less than enthusiastic about his news.

Sam walked in just as she was replacing the phone.

"What's wrong?"

She smiled faintly. He knew her so well. One look at her face and he crossed the room to take her in his arms.

"Ron's been arrested." She shook her head, trying to remember the sergeant's exact words. "That's not right. He's being held for questioning."

"What are we waiting for? Let's go see him."

Her smile deepened. "Did I tell you how much I love you?"

"Not nearly often enough." His hand closed around hers.

Inside the precinct station, Carla's senses were assailed by the noise — the clattering of an old-fashioned typewriter, the cursing, the occasional weeping. The soft crying of a woman caught her attention. She looked around, wanting to help, but Sam touched her arm and reminded her of their purpose.

"Mrs. Hastings? Sergeant Nichols," a thin officer with sparse hair introduced himself before turning to Sam and nodding briefly.

"Where's Ron?" she asked.

"In a holding cell. He's being brought to an interrogation room right now."

His hand on her elbow, Sam started down the hall.

"Sorry, Councilman." Nichols held up a hand. "He asked to see Mrs. Hastings. Nobody else."

She sensed Sam's objection and laid her hand on his arm. "It's all right."

The sergeant led her to a small room and closed the door behind her.

Her heart turned over when she saw Ron slouched in a chair, his head resting on his folded arms. "C'mon, Ron. We're getting you out of here."

He slumped even lower. "It's 'cause of you that I'm in here, preacher lady."

The accusation in his eyes, the bitterness in his voice both hurt. But she wasn't here to have her feelings ruffled. She was here to help Ron. If she could.

She reminded herself that he'd asked for her. "We'll talk later. Let's get out of here first."

He looked as if he wanted to argue, but he followed her out to where Sam waited.

Ron barely acknowledged Sam's presence. He slouched against the wall as Carla signed the papers necessary for his release.

"Thanks," he said once they were outside, but the sneer in his voice said something different.

"You're welcome," Carla returned evenly. She sensed Sam's growing annoyance and tried to smooth things over. "We know you didn't take Samson."

"Then who sicced the cops on me?"

Carla and Sam exchanged glances. It wasn't too hard to figure out who'd given Ron's name to the police. "It doesn't matter," she said.

"It matters to me." He knuckled away a tear. "You give me all this bull about how you believe in me, then you let a bunch of self-righteous jerks from your church get me thrown in jail."

"I didn't let them —"

"You didn't stop them."

She laid a hand on his shoulder. "Let us take you home. Please."

He shrugged off her hand. "I'll get myself home."

"We've lost him," she said to Sam as they watched Ron walk away.

"You don't know that."

"I feel it. Here," she said, placing her hand on her heart. "Did you see the look in his eyes?"

"I saw a kid who's feeling sorry for himself."

"He's got a right. Hauled in for something he didn't do."

"It was for questioning."

"To a fifteen-year-old, it's the same thing. He was just beginning to open up. Now we're right back where he started — a scared kid who thinks the whole world's against him." She pressed her fingers to her eyes, feeling tears being to form.

Sam brushed them away, the pad of his thumb smoothing her cheek. "C'mon," he said gently. "We're going home."

"But we have to —"

"We can't help Ron standing here."

He was right, of course. Only she wasn't at all sure how they could help Ron. Or if they could help him at all.

She rubbed her fingers over her eyes and then read through what she'd written.

Gibberish.

Wadding the paper into a ball, she aimed and threw it. It landed neatly in the trash can.

"Nice shot."

She looked up to find Sam watching her. She smiled in response to his grin. "Thanks. Too bad my sermon isn't as good as my hook shot."

"Can I help?"

She took his hand and rubbed it against her cheek. "You already have."

"Still worrying about Ron?"

She gave a reluctant nod. "I've tried calling him every day. His mom says he's out, but I know he's ducking me."

"Give him time."

Her eyes clouded. "I'm pushing. I know it. It's only because . . ."

"You care so much."

She looked up at him. "Or too much?"

"With you, it's the same thing."

There was no censure in his words or his eyes. Only love.

"We'll find a way to help him," Sam said, tucking a curl behind her ear.

"I hope so. He's so vulnerable."

Ron wasn't the only one, Sam thought. Carla was more vulnerable than any street-smart kid. She led with her heart, never thinking of the cost to herself. And now she was paying the price.

The following evening, Sam studied Carla over the top of the newspaper. He frowned at the weary droop to her mouth.

"Something the matter?"

She looked up. The strained smile on her lips made him more concerned than ever. "Uh uh."

"You're working too hard."

Her smile faltered before she bolstered it up. "There's so much to do —"

"And you have to do it all."

Her smile disappeared altogether. "Someone has to draft the proposal for the city coalition of churches."

"Why does it have to be you?"

"Why shouldn't it be me?"

He had no answer, besides the fact that he didn't want to see her working herself so hard.

"I love you for worrying about me. But there's no need." She skimmed her hand down his cheek. "Really."

He caught her hand and brought it to his lips. She giggled as he nibbled at her fingers. He leered at her with a wicked lift of his eyebrows. "I vant to have my way with you."

"You're nuts."

"Nuts about you." His expression sobered. "You can't do everything."

"Seems like I've heard this song before."

"Seems like I've sung it." He tucked a strand of hair behind her ear. "If so, it's because I love you."

"I know."

"That's a start."

"Maybe we can find a desert island," she said, pressing her lips to his. "Just the two of us."

Her words lingered in his mind for the rest of the evening. He might not be able to scare up a desert island, but he could manage the rest. Just the two of them. Alone. No phones, no one making demands on either of them.

Between his job and the city council meetings, Carla's church duties, volunteering at the shelter, and a host of other things, they struggled to slice out time for themselves. An idea took shape in his mind. He stole one last glance at Carla, more convinced than ever that they both needed time away.

He spent the following day clearing his desk. When he arrived home in the middle of the afternoon, he started packing their bags.

"Are you going on a trip?"

He shook his head. "We're going. I'm

kidnapping you."

"You're what?"

"You heard me. I'm kidnapping you."

"But there's George and Thomas and —"

"Jared's taking care of them."

"My sermon on Sunday — I need to polish it. And I'm supposed to wallpaper the church nursery tomorrow."

"If you polish that sermon any more, you'll be able to see yourself in it. And the nursery can wait. The kids won't mind." While they were talking, he hustled her out to the car.

"How do you know?" she asked, picking up the conversation after he started the car.

"I asked them. They said they liked the wallpaper just like it is."

"You asked a bunch of babies if they liked the wallpaper in the nursery?"

"Sure."

"And they answered you?"

"They said they loved it."

"You're going to have to repent when we get home, you know."

"What for?"

"Lying to your minister. That's a serious sin."

"Think she'll forgive me?"

"She might." She gave him a stern look. "If she thought you were truly sorry."

"What would it take to convince her?"

She leaned across the seat to kiss his cheek. "Oh, I'll think of something."

He slanted her a grin. "I can't wait."

"One more thing."

"What's that?"

"Kidnapping's against the law."

"You going to turn me in?"

"Depends."

"On what?"

"Where you're taking me."

"Sorry. That's classified."

She settled back in the seat. "Okay."

"That's it? Okay?"

"As long as you're the one doing the kidnapping, I'll go willingly."

"Good. Otherwise I'd have to use force."

"Sounds interesting. What kind of force did you have in mind?"

He leaned over to kiss her. "This kind."

"I like the way you think." She settled back to enjoy the ride. At some point she must have drifted off, because when she awoke, the car was parked in front of a log cabin.

Sam opened the door for her. "Sleeping Beauty, your castle awaits."

She took a moment to look around. Individual cabins were scattered randomly around a centrally located office and a restaurant. Inside their cabin, she gave a little cry of delight. Decorated in sea and sand tones, with casual furniture and a hooked rug, the cabin promised quiet, comfort, and privacy. A fully equipped kitchen ensured that they wouldn't have to leave the cabin unless they chose to.

She lifted a window and inhaled sharply. The tangy scent of the ocean beckoned to her. She turned to Sam. "How did you know I needed this?"

Gently he traced the shadows under her eyes. "These told me."

She twined her fingers with his, bringing his knuckles to her lips. "Remind me to tell you later that I love you."

"Count on it."

Without bothering to unpack, they headed to the beach. A breeze caught her hair, blowing tendrils across her face. She didn't push it away, enjoying the unaccustomed freedom. Here she was free to be Carla, rather than Reverend Hastings.

Whitewashed pieces of driftwood jutted from the sand. She rolled up her jeans, kicked off her sneakers, and waded into the ocean. Waves lapped around her feet, nipping at her ankles. The water was cold this late in the day, but she didn't care. She laughed at the antics of a seagull as it dived after its prey.

"Last one in is a rotten egg," she called to Sam.

He unlaced his shoes and waded out to join her. "Are you trying to freeze us, woman?"

"It feels great," she said.

"Yeah. If you're into freezing to death."

She kicked up some water, splashing him.

"This means war." He retaliated in kind until they were both soaked and laughing so hard they could barely stand.

The breeze picked up, gusting around them. Goosebumps scattered over Carla's skin as the wind plastered her shirt to her back. Her wet jeans dragged at her as she started back to shore. She tripped, nearly falling. He scooped her up in his arms and carried her, pausing occasionally to groan exaggeratedly under her weight.

She punched him lightly on the shoulder. "Out of shape, huh, Hastings?"

"No way." To prove it, he slung her over his shoulder, carrying her the rest of the way to the cabin.

She giggled, pounding on his back.

"Hit the showers," he ordered with a mock growl when they reached the cabin.

She saluted smartly. "Aye, aye, sir."

Sam smiled as she disappeared into the

bathroom, singing slightly off-key. Within a few minutes, the sound of the shower drowned out her voice.

It was good to see her happy, he thought, shedding his own wet clothing. They both needed a break. She'd been so wrapped up in dealing with the problems of her congregation that she'd scarcely taken time to eat. When Samson had been stolen, she had spent more time than ever with Ethan and Maude, trying to reassure them.

With no phone, they'd be out of reach. Three days alone together. He intended to make the most of it.

Sam glanced at his watch. Eight more hours before they needed to start home. Eight more hours before reality, with all its attendant responsibilities and duties, once again intruded on them. Eight more hours alone with Carla.

The weekend had been all that he'd hoped . . . and more. Seeing Carla relaxed and happy was worth all the juggling and rearranging of schedules. Her eyes had lost the shadows that had underscored them for the past couple of weeks. They sparkled with life and vitality.

He listened as the shower switched off. He shook away his melancholy. Now was for them. And he intended to make the most of every hour, every minute before they had to return.

After breakfast, he grabbed her hand. "Race you to the beach."

They scampered down the grassy slope to the beach, laughing as they slipped and skidded to the bottom.

"Come on! The water's gorgeous," Carla called, shedding her clothes as she raced to the water.

Sam followed more slowly, unable to drag his gaze away from her. She was more beautiful than ever. The sun had turned her skin the color of pale honey and streaked her hair with light. The pink bathing suit hugged her curves in a way that made it hard for him to remember that she was a preacher lady.

"What are you waiting for?" she shouted above the roar of the ocean.

Grinning, he stripped off his jeans and shirt and joined her in the water.

They romped in the ocean like children given an unexpected holiday from school, splashing, frolicking, and diving in the water. He smacked his hand on the surface, showering her with a gush of water. She pounced on him, but he caught her by the waist, pulling her under. Kicking away from him, she pushed her way to the top, sputtering, her hair plastered to her face. She grabbed him by the shoulders and tried to dunk him, but he darted away, disappearing underwater. She scanned the water for him, growing alarmed until she felt strong hands grabbing at her ankles. Before she could react, he'd pulled her under with him. He caught her lips with his. Slowly they rose to the surface, still locked together in the kiss.

When they had exhausted themselves in the water, they ran, laughing, to collapse on the sand. He tossed her a towel, which she tied like a sarong around her waist. Stretched out on his towel, he watched over the rim of his sunglasses as she built a sand castle, complete with turrets and drawbridge, her lip caught between her teeth as she concentrated on her task.

When a wave washed away her castle, she didn't appear upset. She dug her toes in the wet sand and laughed as water filled the imprints left by her feet. Then she stretched out on her towel.

He stroked the ebony hair that lay like wet silk around her shoulders before brushing it aside to press a kiss to the sweet curve of her neck. She turned in his arms so her lips met his.

The wind freshened, chilling their still-damp skin. The sky, moments ago gold and blue, darkened to gunmetal. The sun lowered, shadowing the day still further.

Reluctantly he pulled his watch from the pocket of his jeans. "It's time to go."

She nodded.

Silently they began gathering up their clothes and towels. At the cabin, they washed off the salt and sand, packed their bags, and loaded the car.

Pulling out of the driveway, Sam took one last look at the cabin. "We'll come back."

Her hand found his. "Soon."

The ride home passed quietly as neither of them felt compelled to talk. The silence was comfortable, unbroken save for the occasional whisper of love.

When he pulled into the driveway, Sam was jolted to see Jared sitting on the front porch. *Something was wrong.* It didn't take a genius to read the worry in the boy's eyes or the dejection in the droop of his shoulders. Sam climbed out of the car and then went around to open Carla's door. One glance at her face told him she recognized something was wrong too.

Jared rose and crossed the yard. "Carla, Sam . . ." He looked from one to the other.

"What is it?" she asked.

"George is gone."

CHAPTER SEVEN

"We'll do the best we can, Mr. Hastings. But . . ." The police officer let the implication trail off politely.

"You don't expect to find him, do you?"

The officer shook his head regretfully. "It's like we told you before. A missing dog . . . you understand."

"Yeah. I understand."

After answering a few more questions, he saw the police off and turned back to Carla. He knew how discouraged she must feel. He felt pretty dismal himself. He had no doubt that George had been stolen by the same person responsible for taking the other dogs. And they were no closer to finding that person than they had been weeks ago.

He gripped Carla's hand. "We'll find him."

Her fingers curled inside his. "I know."

Bleakly Sam looked out the window. As if the weather sensed his mood, rain slashed the sky in ragged sheets of gray. Shafts of lightning carved paths of fire through the downpour. The magical days at the beach seemed light-years away instead of mere hours.

They didn't even make a pretense of eating dinner.

Hours later, after they'd gone to bed, he heard Carla slip out. He watched as she crossed the room to sit on the window seat. In the darkness, she was little more than a silhouette outlined against the glow created by shafts of moonlight. He went to her. He didn't need to say anything. He simply held her. It was enough.

For both of them.

The following day, he went through the motions at work, his mind elsewhere.

The intercom buzzed, and Sarah's voice came over the line. "Sam, there's a call for you. Line one."

He picked up the phone.

"Sam?"

Upon hearing his father's voice, he stared at the receiver. Although relations had improved between himself and his parents, his father rarely called, and never at work.

"Your mother told me about George. Is there anything I can do?"

Sam paused, not sure he'd heard correctly. His father was asking if he could help because a dog was missing?

"Sam, are you there?"

"Sorry."

"I asked if there was anything I could do to help. If it's a question of ransom . . ."

Disappointment surged through him. His father hadn't changed after all. He thought everything could be solved by throwing money at it. Sam bit back a sigh of disappointment. So great was his frustration that he almost missed Gerald's next words.

"Maybe we could offer a reward."

Sam frowned at the uncertainty in his father's voice. Gerald Hastings was never uncertain about anything. Until now.

For the first time since he'd picked up the phone, Sam listened with his heart instead of his ears. Now he heard the concern behind the offer of money. His father was helping in the only way he knew how.

"There haven't been any calls about ransom. But I appreciate the thought."

"Well, in that case . . ." The gruffness was back, but Sam wasn't fooled this time. "Uh, Sam?"

"Yes?"

"Carla — She's a fine woman."

Sam swallowed his surprise. "Yes, she is."

"About George. You'll let us know if — when — you find him?"

"Right away. Dad?" Sam stopped, marveling that he didn't stumble over the unfamiliar word.

"What . . . son?" The pause was slight but present nonetheless.

Apparently he wasn't the only one who felt awkward, Sam reflected.

"Thanks for calling."

After exchanging good-byes, they hung up.

Sam stared at the phone. A miracle had just occurred.

They'd scarcely slept the night before. It showed in Sam's face, Carla thought, studying him. He wore a ragged edge of fatigue that tugged at her heart and her conscience. She knew he was more worried than he let on. She also knew he was putting on a good front for her sake.

Slipping her arms around his waist, she laid her head on his shoulder. "I love you." She felt his shuddering breath. Automatically she tightened her hold.

"How did I ever survive without you?"

"Who said you did?"

To her relief, he chuckled. It was a small one, but it filled her with relief just the same.

She slipped her hand in his. "Sit down. I'm fixing you breakfast, and you're going to eat every bite of it."

"Yes, ma'am," he said.

She whipped eggs and milk together. She was pouring the mixture into an omelet pan when she heard a noise at the kitchen door. Probably Jared, she thought with a faint smile. He frequently showed up for breakfast on Saturday mornings. Wiping her hands on her jeans, she opened the door.

"George!"

The dog limped inside, favoring his right side.

Not caring about the dirt and blood that matted the dog's coat, Carla hugged him to her. "It's okay, boy," she whispered. "You're home now."

He whimpered when she ran her hands over his side.

"What have they done to you?"

Sam nudged her aside and gently lifted one of George's paws to examine it. The pads were raw and bleeding. "He must have traveled a couple of hundred miles."

"Just to get home."

"Yeah." He gathered the dog in his arms. "Let's get him to the vet."

She hurried to open the door for them, swiping at the tears that trekked down her cheeks. She climbed into the backseat, where Sam settled George by her side.

Holding George's head in her lap during the ride, she prayed.

John Castleton, a vet and a friend, took one look at George and gestured for Sam to take him into the operating room. Carla started to follow, but John slipped his hand onto her shoulder. "Wait here. Please."

Reluctantly she did as he said. When Sam returned, she stood. "How —"

"We don't know yet."

"So we wait."

He took her hand. "We wait."

She counted the tiles on the floor and then shifted her gaze to the ceiling. Anything to keep her eyes from the clock, where the minute hand seemed to have stopped completely.

She clenched the arms of her chair more tightly when John made a hurried trip through the lobby, a grim expression in his eyes. Her knuckles whitened under the pressure until Sam gently pried her hands loose. He folded her hands in his and held them. He didn't say anything. He was simply there. Quietly there. Just as he'd been throughout the ordeal.

When John reappeared, Carla jumped up.

John gave a tired smile. "George is going to be all right. How he managed to get as far as he did, I'll never know."

"Can we see him?" she asked.

"He's sedated right now." John smiled slightly. "But you can see him."

Carla hurried into the operating room.

Sam stayed behind, wanting to talk with John privately.

"What aren't you telling us?"

John held up a .38 bullet. "I dug this out of his side." His lips compressed into a narrow line. "I've spent most of my life treating sick animals. When I see something like this, I start thinking about hanging the scum responsible."

"So do I."

"Are you going to tell Carla?"

"I have to. She deserves to know the truth."

"Yeah. You're right." John clapped Sam on the back. "You're lucky, old buddy. You got yourself one special lady there."

For the first time in two days, Sam grinned. John was right. He was lucky.

When they brought George home three days later, Jared was there. Sam knew the boy felt responsible for what had happened.

When Jared knelt to hug the dog, there were tears in his eyes. "We're gonna pamper you. Only steak and prime rib bones from now on."

George must have understood, for he barked enthusiastically.

Sam and Carla exchanged smiles. They spent the rest of the day spoiling George, finally sending Jared home after dark.

The next day Ron showed up, carrying a large, greasy sack. "I, uh, heard George was back. I brought him this." He dug in the sack, producing the biggest bone Carla had ever seen.

George spied the bone and gave a yelp.

"You're a hit," Carla said to Ron, who continued standing in the doorway. She tugged on his arm. "Come on in. You can help us celebrate."

Ron gave her an uneasy look. "I'd better not stay. I just wanted to apologize. I acted like a real jerk the other day. I was feeling pretty sorry for myself, but I shouldn't have dumped on you like that."

"That's what friends are for," she said.

"Take it easy, George," Sam cautioned as the dog all but attacked the bone. "You're still recovering."

George turned his attention to Ron and licked his face.

"I don't think George knows he's been sick," the boy said, burying his face in the dog's fur.

"I think you're right."

Something was bothering Sam.

Carla knew it. Moreover, she *felt* it. She'd seen it in his eyes when he returned home last night. She knew he was still worried about the missing dogs and the threat to her, but she sensed this was something different. Something to do with work.

When the idea came to her, she picked up the phone.

"A delivery came for you, Sam," Sarah said, looking up from her computer.

"Deal with it, will you?"

"Can't." She gestured to her desk, which was piled high with papers. "Too busy. I told him to put it in your office."

Sam scowled as he slammed the door to the reception area behind him. He didn't have time to open mail. A business lunch had kept him later than he'd expected. He had two contracts to rough out plus a proposal for the city council to prepare.

His scowl intensified as he acknowledged the real cause behind his short temper. He'd been approached about designing the San Diego Arts and Humanities Center. It would represent the biggest challenge of his career. And he had turned it down. He couldn't leave Carla. Not until the dogs were found and the threat to her was over.

He pushed the images of possible designs for the center from his mind as he stepped inside his office. What was with Sarah, anyway? It was her job to take care of deliveries. Maybe he'd been working her too hard. Maybe . . .

A profusion of balloons filled the room. He wiped his eyes, certain he was hallucinating. He looked again. The balloons were still there, a kaleidoscope of color gently bobbing around the room.

How did . . .

Carla.

He pulled a neon yellow balloon down and read the message attached to it: *Roses are red, violets are blue, my heart will always belong to you.*

Each balloon held a similar message. Some were downright suggestive. Others were hilarious. All had the same effect. By the time Sam finished reading them, he was grinning widely.

She'd done it again.

Turned his world upside down. And inside out. Swept away the petty worries that dragged him down. He was still smiling as he picked up the phone, intending to call her. Abruptly he put it down.

Some things had to be done in person.

The evening was touched with magic. Or at least it was until the call came. She felt the change in Sam immediately. Heard it in his voice.

"I'm sorry," Sam said. "It's like I told you yesterday. I can't leave right now. If you could hold off for a week — maybe two . . ."

The person at the other end of the line must have said something, for Sam's voice trailed off. "No. I'm afraid it won't work," he said at last. "Yeah. I'm sorry too."

The receiver clicked into place.

"Who was that?"

Sam looked up. "Dick Peterson wanted me to scope out a site for the new Arts and Humanities Center in San Diego. If it looks all right, he wants an estimate by next week."

"So why did you say no?"

He gave her a suggestive glance and twirled an imaginary mustache. "I can't keep away from you that long." The smile on his lips didn't touch his eyes. They were dark with regret.

Suddenly it made sense. Why he'd turned down a job he'd been talking about for months.

"It's because you're worried about me,

isn't it? Isn't it?" she persisted when he didn't answer.

He kissed her lightly. "It's only a job."

"A job you'd give your right arm for."

He didn't deny it. "There'll be others."

"But not like this. You've wanted a chance at that center ever since you heard about it." She saw the truth in his eyes. "Sam, I don't need you hovering over me." She paused, letting her words sink in. "I need a husband, not a baby-sitter."

"The truck —"

"Didn't hit me. I'm fine."

"I don't like the idea of leaving you alone."

"I won't be alone. George is almost recovered. And there's Thomas."

Sam groaned. "The only danger anyone would be in from George is being licked to death. And Thomas would sleep through a break-in."

Carla picked up the phone and held it out to him. "Do you want to call or shall I?"

"You're impossible."

"Yeah," she said, her lips curving in satisfaction. "And you love me for it."

"You're right."

She listened while he made the arrangements.

"If I leave tomorrow morning, I'll be back by the evening of the next day at the latest," he said after hanging up.

"Then let's make the most of tonight."

Saying good-bye to Sam was harder than she'd imagined. It was the first time they'd been apart since their marriage.

"I don't have to go," Sam said gently, his thumb wiping away a tear that spilled over and trickled down her cheek.

"And waste a perfectly wonderful good-bye scene? No way." She kissed him and reminded herself that this had been her idea after all. "Call when you get in and I'll pick you up."

"It'll probably be late. I'll call a cab."

"You do and I'll —"

He cut off the rest of the threat by covering her lips with his own.

She took her time on the drive home. Returning to an empty house left her feeling vaguely depressed. Her lips kicked up at the corners as she thought about George and Thomas. She wouldn't be alone.

The phone was ringing when she walked in. Nearly tripping over Thomas, she raced to answer it.

"Carla?"

Maude's voice sounded old, Carla thought with a pang. Old and defeated. That wasn't like Maude, who'd survived hip surgery at eighty-plus years old without losing her spunk.

"Hi, Maude."

"I'm sorry to bother you. I was just wondering if there was any word . . . about Samson."

"Not yet. I'll let you know as soon as there is." Carla tried to think of something that would take Maude's mind off her missing pet. "Why don't I come over? I just got the pictures back from the church dance, and I thought you and Ethan might like to see them."

"If you don't mind, dear, maybe we could make it another time. I'm feeling a little peaked."

"If you're sure . . ."

"Thanks, honey. I'll talk to you later."

Frowning, Carla replaced the receiver.

She had to do something. She'd talked to Mrs. Miller yesterday. The old lady was more upset about Collette than ever. So was Thelma. Finding the dogs wasn't just a matter of returning stolen pets; it was giving people back their lives.

She reviewed what they knew. People's pets were missing. A research lab was located nearby. So far they hadn't found a connection, but that didn't mean one didn't exist. She looked up the address and scribbled some directions on an envelope.

Her promise to Sam nagged at her. But, she reasoned, she didn't intend to do anything dangerous. All she planned was to visit the lab, maybe ask a few questions. After convincing herself that she was doing the right thing, she spent the rest of the day talking herself out of it.

The following morning, she'd settled on a compromise. She'd visit the lab before picking Sam up at the airport. If she learned anything, she'd share it with him. If not, well, they wouldn't be any worse off than they were before.

She turned on the ignition. Nothing.

"Not today, Emma," she prayed aloud. "Please, not today."

The car, which she'd named after her grandmother, remained stubbornly quiet. She eyed Sam's car. He'd encouraged her often enough in the past to use it.

Finding the lab wasn't hard. A niggling of doubt about what she was about to do crawled through her mind. With Maude's dejected voice still fresh in her memory, she pushed her uncertainty away. She was here to help her friends. Sam couldn't object to that. She took a deep breath and opened the car door.

"Can you please tell me who's in charge?"

she said once she was inside the lab.

A guard, who looked like he spent most of his time working out in a gym, gave her a bored look. "Mr. Garrity. But he's out."

"When do you think he'll be back?"

He shrugged. "Your guess is as good as mine."

She settled on a vinyl chair.

The muscle-bound guard answered the phone.

"Yes, sir," she heard him say. "Right away." When he disappeared down a hallway, she decided to take a chance and find Garrity's office on her own.

The glass-fronted door with Garrity's name on it opened when she pushed against it. Her conscience gave her a few qualms as she searched Garrity's desk. She hardened herself against it as she remembered the despair in Maude's voice. Just when she was about to give up, she saw it. A telephone number scrawled on the corner of a page from a notebook. She stared at it disbelievingly, certain she must have misread the digits. Even as she took a second look, she knew she hadn't been mistaken. She'd found the connection.

She only wished she didn't feel so depressed over it.

■ ■ ■ ■

A thin drizzle was falling, turning the sky to a murky gray, as she pulled up in front of the house. She squinted as she tried to see through the rain before settling back in the seat, preparing to wait. Checking her watch, she figured she'd have just enough time to tail her man for an hour and see if he might lead her to the dogs before she picked Sam up at the airport.

For a moment she considered confronting him. Convince him to give back the dogs and . . . And what? she asked herself. What was to keep him from denying the whole thing? She had no evidence against him — just a phone number scrawled on a piece of paper. She was no lawyer, but she knew enough to realize that this bit of evidence wouldn't stand up in a court of law. She'd only tip him off, then they might never find the dogs.

Her musings were cut short when the door opened and he walked out, his head bent against the rain. She ducked down and heard an engine sputter then catch. She waited for a few moments before starting Sam's car.

Following her quarry wasn't difficult. He

drove slowly, apparently not wanting to attract any attention. She followed well behind, keeping at least a car or two between them. When the rain stopped, a dense fog provided cover.

He kept to the main roads for more than an hour. When he pulled off a narrow side road, she hesitated. If she followed him, she risked detection. If she didn't, she might lose him.

When a few minutes had passed, she turned. The car bumped and bounced its way over the rutted lane until it ended abruptly. Through the mist she saw a building.

It was as gray as the fog-laden sky. She parked Sam's car behind a stand of pines and approached on foot. Leaves slick from the recent rain covered the ground, making walking treacherous. She picked her way carefully until she was standing outside a window.

She scurried for cover as a door whined, moving on its hinges. She had barely ducked behind a clump of bushes when he reappeared. She heard the engine flare to life and then fade into the distance. Now was her chance to search the building. Standing on tiptoe, she attempted to peer in a window, but a film of dirt and dust coating the glass obscured her vision. She rubbed at the glass with her sleeve, but she only succeeded in smearing the grime.

She didn't much like the idea of entering an unfamiliar place when she had no idea who — or what — might be waiting for her, but she didn't have a choice. She pushed on the door, surprised when it gave way. She took a moment to let her eyes adjust to the dimness before she looked around, taking stock of her surroundings. Cinder block walls, concrete floors, mesh wire-covered windows. The place was a prison.

A faint sound snagged her attention.

Her eyes not fully accustomed to the shadowy interior, she squinted to the far corner where the sound seemed to originate. When her vision focused, she saw a bank of cages.

Her caution fled as she ran to them. "Grover Cleveland." Her gaze strayed to the next cage. "Samson."

Next to Samson was Collette. Then Charlie. She counted a dozen other dogs. She knelt by each cage in turn, trying to reach through the wire to comfort the dogs. To her surprise, they didn't look frightened but strangely lethargic, their eyes glazed and dull.

It took her a moment to understand the

significance of their lack of responsiveness. They'd been drugged.

She stood, anger warring with disbelief. What kind of monster kept helpless animals drugged and caged? She studied the dogs. They all appeared well fed. She started noticing other things as well. The cages, though cold and barren, were scrupulously clean. The dogs appeared to be well cared for. At least the thief wasn't completely heartless, she decided, changing her opinion a bit.

She had just stretched her arm through a cage to pet Samson when the squeak of hinges protesting against infrequent use caused her to freeze.

CHAPTER EIGHT

Wildly she looked around for some kind of cover. There was nothing. Nothing except the cages. A trickle of sweat skated down her back, chilling her. Or was it fear? She had no time to decide as the door groaned its way open. She stood, not wanting to be caught on her hands and knees. Lifting her chin, she braced her feet and planted her hands on her hips. She didn't intend to look scared.

Even though she was.

The shock on his face would have made her laugh at any other time. But not now. She heard his swift intake of breath. She'd succeeded in surprising him. Maybe she could turn it to her advantage. Heaven knew she needed it. He stood between her and the door.

"Surprised to see me?" Martin asked after long moments had passed.

"No."

"You wouldn't be, would you? Gram always said you were smart. I'm sorry you found us, Reverend Hastings," he said, closing the distance between them. "You're too curious for your own good. Now . . ."

"Now what?"

"I'm sorry. For both of us."

There was no anger in his voice, only regret. That gave her hope. He didn't like what he was doing. She was sure of it. If only she could make him see that as well.

He reached inside his boot and pulled something out. A knife gleamed softly in the faint light. It looked incongruous in Martin's hands — hands he had dedicated to healing. She was smart enough to be afraid. Still, she refused to give way to her fear.

"Aren't you scared at all?"

She started to deny it, but she settled on the truth. "Yes."

He gave her a look of admiration, one that did nothing to lessen the grim intent in his eyes as he stroked the blade of the knife against his sleeve. "You had to keep poking your nose into it, didn't you? You couldn't leave it alone."

"You . . ." Fear jammed in her throat as he rubbed the knife back and forth, the faint light catching the movement. She tried to swallow and found she couldn't. She wet her lips and tried again. She couldn't outrun or outfight Martin. She had to make him see what she saw in him so plainly. "You don't like hurting people."

"No." The word, uttered in a hoarse voice, gave her hope.

"You hurt a lot of people when you took their pets."

"They're just dogs. *Dogs.*"

"Your grandmother, Mrs. Miller, the Sandbergs — they love those dogs."

"They'll get others. Come on, Reverend. What are a few dogs when compared to saving lives? Human lives? Do you know what's being done with medical research? Do you understand the difference we can make if we have the subjects to experiment on?"

"These aren't subjects," she said. "They're people's pets." She bent to pet Grover Cleveland through the bars of his cage. "You know how your grandmother dotes on him. How could you take him away from her?"

"I had to."

"But why —"

He laughed shortly. "Whatever you think of me, Reverend, I'm not stupid. If I hadn't taken Grover Cleveland, it would have looked suspicious."

"It's not too late to take them back. I'll help you. We'll explain —"

"Explain what?"

"Why you did it. We'll make everyone understand."

He laughed shortly. "You're dreaming."

She tried another tack. She knew Martin wasn't heartless. She had to find a way to appeal to his conscience. "If you really wanted to help people, you'd find another way."

"What way is that?"

She had no answer for that. Not now. Not when he continued to caress the knife. "It wasn't your choice to make," she said at last.

"Whose choice was it? Medical research labs need animals to test new drugs, new theories. I supply them with the means to do it. How can that be wrong?"

The passion in his voice convinced her that he meant every word he said. The knife point, shimmering in the dim light, underscored his intensity.

In one swift movement, he caught her around the throat, the flat of the knife smooth against her skin.

She stifled the urge to flinch. "You don't want to do this, Martin. *Think.* Think what it'll do to your grandmother. Think what it'll do to you."

The pressure at her neck eased ever so slightly, and she pressed her advantage.

"So far all you've done is kidnap a few dogs. They can be returned. Nothing that can't be fixed. But if you . . ." She took a deep breath. "If you do this, nothing's going to help you."

"I'm real sorry, Reverend Hastings. But it's too late," he said, the polite words in ludicrous contrast to the knife held to her neck. "If I let you go, then you'll tell everyone. I can't let you do that."

"Everyone knows already," she said, praying she was right. When Sam returned home . . .

Sam. She was late picking him up. He was probably furious with her. She'd promised she wouldn't go off on her own. Right now her reasons for doing just that sounded pretty weak.

If he saw her scribbled directions to the research lab . . . *If* he figured out about Martin . . . *If* . . . The word taunted her with all its possibilities. She tried to remember.

"My husband, your grandmother, the people at the lab. If . . ." There was that word again. "If you hurt me, you'll spend the rest of your life in jail. You don't want that. Think what it'll do to your grandmother."

"If I let you go, I'll still go to jail."

She chose her words carefully. "Yes. You will. But it'll only be for a short time. You're still young. And when you get out, you can —"

"I can't be a doctor."

"You don't know that."

He looked disappointed in her. "C'mon, Reverend. You and I both know the score."

"Okay. So maybe you can't. But there are lots of other things you can do."

"All I've ever wanted is to be a doctor. From the time I was six years old I knew what I was going to be when I grew up. That's the only thing that mattered. I watched my mother die a day at a time from cancer. I promised myself I'd find a way to prevent it from happening to other people."

"There are a lot of things you can do. Medical technician. Lab assistant."

"Technician. Assistant." He practically spat the words. "I want to be a doctor. I'd be a good one too. With the right research, I could save lives. Lots of lives."

"How can you say you want to be a doctor in one breath and then kill me with the next? Doctors heal. They don't kill."

"No, they don't." His sigh shivered over her. He lowered his arm, releasing her as he dropped the knife.

She scooted away.

"I can't hurt you." He gave a faint smile. "But you knew that, didn't you?"

The whoosh of breath startled her until she realized it came from her. Cautiously she stooped to pick up the knife. "It's going to be all right." She looked at the steel blade in her hand before throwing it as far as she could.

The door grumbled its way open again. A draft of cool air hit her back. She turned as she heard the slap of feet against the concrete, squinting to make out the figure shrouded in shadows. When recognition came, she slammed her hand over her mouth. She was mistaken. She had to be. She looked again and knew she wasn't.

When Carla didn't show up at the airport, Sam wasn't worried. She'd probably been caught in traffic. He collected his luggage, settled into a chair, and opened his briefcase. He'd spend the time going over the rough contract he and Dick Peterson had hammered out yesterday.

When she didn't arrive after an hour, he called. The answering machine replayed its message. Sam drummed his fingers against the counter. "Darn it, Carla. Pick up." When it became clear that no answer was forthcoming, he left a message that he'd take a cab home.

She had just gone out. No big deal. There were a dozen reasons why she could have been held up. There was no reason for the hair at the nape of his neck to prick up.

He hailed a cab. "There's an extra twenty in it for you if you get me there fast," he said, giving the driver the address.

The cabdriver flashed him a big grin. "You got it, buddy."

It was a good thing he was used to rough rides, Sam thought, gripping the door handle as the cab raced along the freeway.

Deliberately he pushed any worries about Carla to the back of his mind and remembered last night. When he'd called her to tell her that he'd gotten the job, her yell of delight had nearly destroyed his eardrums. A small smile played at his lips as he remembered the rest of the conversation.

"I'll be home tomorrow afternoon." He gave her the flight number and arrival time.

"I'll be there." Her voice turned low and husky. "I love you."

"Not as much as I love you."

His spirits soared when he saw Emma parked in the driveway. Carla was home. She'd probably been called away when he'd phoned. Everything was all right. The rapid-fire beat of his heart slowed. He paid the fare, adding a generous tip in addition to the promised twenty.

His fingers fumbled as he inserted the key in the door. "Carla! Where were you? I tried calling . . ."

There was no answering sound of footsteps, unless he counted the soft slap of Thomas' paws against the linoleum as he pattered into the room.

The familiar scents of home — rose potpourri, lemon furniture polish — wrapped themselves around him. Things appeared so ordinary that he could almost believe nothing was wrong.

Almost.

He tried again. "Carla?"

The silence settled over him with depressing finality. He'd hoped — prayed — she'd returned while he was en route.

George wandered into the room.

"Where is she, boy?"

The dog woofed as Thomas swished between Sam's legs.

He walked back outside to look at Emma. Why hadn't she taken her car? It didn't take long to find the problem. The battery was dead. He called a neighbor, and they jump started the car. Still no sign of Carla.

When the phone rang, he grabbed for it. "Carla?"

"Sam?"

Disappointment clogged his throat when he recognized Pete Hammond's voice. "Yeah, Pete. What can I do for you?"

"Sorry to call you at home. I tried the office, but you weren't there. Figured you were home with that pretty wife of yours." Pete laughed. When Sam didn't respond, he continued, "Listen, about that preschool project, what do you say we get together and try to hammer out some kind of deal?"

At any other time Sam would have jumped at a chance to reach a compromise with the senior member of the city council to obtain funds for a preschool for low-income families, but not today. Not when his gut was twisted into a pretzel.

"Sam, you there?"

Pete's voice, edged with impatience, jerked him back to the present. "Yeah."

"What about it?"

"Listen, Pete, I've got something I have to do. Catch you later."

"I haven't finished," Pete protested.

"But I have," Sam said and hung up. He wanted the line clear in case Carla called.

Rather than waste time, he opened his briefcase and pulled out the contract awaiting his attention. But his eyes refused to focus on the words, a condition he wanted to blame on the fine print rather than his inability to concentrate. He made a pretense of looking at the contract before picking up the phone.

"I'm sorry. We haven't seen Carla since Sunday," Maude said. "But I talked to her yesterday."

He grabbed on to that. "Was she okay?"

"She sounded fine. Is there anything wrong?"

"Did you talk about anything special?"

"I just asked if there'd been any news about Samson or the other dogs."

The feeling in his gut tightened.

"Thanks, Maude. Say hi to Ethan for me, okay?" After another few minutes of assuring her that Carla was probably just out visiting someone, he said good-bye and dialed the next number.

"Thanks anyway, Mom," he said upon hearing that his mother hadn't seen Carla. The word was easier to say than he'd feared it would be. "I'll call when I find her."

Six calls later, he was no nearer to locating her. Battling back the panic that threatened to take over, he picked up the phone and started the round of calls again. He didn't stop with the likely places. He phoned every person he could think of who might know where Carla was. Even as he dialed the next number, he knew it was futile. He was only spinning out the process, delaying facing what his gut told him.

"Thank you, Mrs. Miller," he said upon hearing the expected negative answer in response to his question. "Yes, I'll let you know when I find her."

Sam cupped his hand around the receiver, holding it tightly against him as he tried to think. *Think.* The word taunted him as a series of possibilities flashed through his mind, each more grim than the last. He pulled the plug on his imagination, which had shifted into overdrive, and concentrated on what to do next.

The only trouble was, he didn't have a clue.

The shelter. That was it. She'd probably gone over there, lost track of time, and . . . He started dialing.

The buzzing sound of a busy signal droned in his ear.

Too impatient to wait and try again, he drove to the shelter. He broke every speed limit on the way, uncaring of everything but finding Carla.

"Sorry, Sam," Tom Beringer, the shelter's director, said. "We haven't seen her in a couple of days."

Sam's uneasiness came back in full force. The alarm bells ringing in his head wouldn't be ignored any longer. He didn't remember walking back outside, and he looked around in surprise when he saw Emma parked by the curb.

"Where are you, Carla?" The words came out as a whispered prayer.

But the rough sigh of the wind was his only answer.

He forced himself to admit what he'd refused to acknowledge until now: Carla was missing.

At home once more, he started going through the papers on her desk. Notes for Sunday's sermon. A grocery list. Names of possible candidates for the scholarship fund. Despite his worry, he smiled when he saw the happy face she'd drawn beside Ron and Jared's names. His smile faded as he turned up another page and the address of the research lab, with hastily scrawled directions, jumped out at him.

The research lab. Garrity. And Dax. He closed his eyes, picturing a confrontation between Carla and Dax. She wouldn't have been so foolish to go there by herself. Would she? Even as he posed the question, he knew the answer.

He drew in a breath — not quite steadily — and then looked at his watch. Only seconds had passed. Not the hours he'd thought. Only seconds, and his world had suddenly teetered off its axis, spinning dizzily.

"No . . ." The denial hung in the air. He looked around, surprised to find that he was alone. He must have uttered the word, although he had no recollection of saying anything.

He drove with scant attention to the rush hour traffic. Finding Carla was all that mattered. With any luck, she'd still be at the lab. He'd hustle her out of there, read her the riot act for going off on her own, and hold her to him, kissing her over and over — not necessarily in that order.

The lab was as he'd remembered. Gray, squat, and isolated. And no sign of his car. He didn't know how much he'd been praying that Carla would be there — safe and well — until he saw the nearly empty parking lot.

Still, someone might have seen her. He held on to that.

Inside, he didn't bother announcing himself. "Where is she?"

Dax looked up, a smirk on his face. "Who?"

"My wife."

The smirk grew wider. "Good-looking babe with dark hair?"

Sam held on to his temper. "Yeah. Seen her?"

"Maybe."

He grabbed the guard by his shirt, hauling him to his feet. "When?"

"This morning."

"She say where she was going?"

"She didn't say nothing. I didn't even see her go. Hey," Dax called as Sam started toward the rear office. "You can't go back there."

"Yeah? Watch me." When Dax blocked the door, Sam pushed his way past. "Do yourself a favor, buddy, and get out of my way."

"Yeah?"

"Yeah." Something in Sam's voice must have convinced the security guard that he meant what he said, for Dax backed up. "Where's Garrity?"

"Out."

"Not good enough."

Dax shrugged. "Can't help it, man. It's the truth. Garrity's not here."

Sam headed to Garrity's office. Inside, he shut the door, blocking out the sound of Dax's protests. A search through Garrity's desk revealed nothing of interest. He started to close the center drawer when it caught on something. He pulled out the drawer and turned it over. A sheet of paper was taped to the bottom. On it he found a scrawled list of numbers — no, dates. He did some quick calculations — the dates indicated when the dogs had been stolen.

He flipped through a Rolodex on Garrity's desk.

When Garrity walked in, Sam pulled out the list of dates. "Don't bother denying it — I know you're using stolen animals. The only question is, are you the thief or are you just the receiver?"

The older man tried to bluster his way out of it. "You're crazy."

"Try again."

"You've no right coming in here —"

Sam picked up the phone. "Let's call the police and see what they say about my rights."

"Wait. Maybe I have received a few animals without the proper paperwork, but that doesn't mean —"

"Save it. Just tell me where the animals are stored."

"I don't know. That's the truth," Garrity said when Sam started toward him. "All I have is a number."

"Get it."

"If I cooperate —" A look at Sam's face must have convinced Garrity not to try to cut a deal. "Okay, okay. Just do what you have to." He was already pulling out a pocket-size notebook. He opened it up and shoved it toward Sam. "Here. Take it."

Sam tore the paper out. "You better not be jerking my chain." He glanced at the number. It was familiar. He frowned, trying to place it. When he did, he swore softly.

CHAPTER NINE

"Jerry?"

Carla winced at the sound of her voice, a squeak of sound that betrayed just how frightened she was.

"That's right. Surprised to see me?" Jerry Foster, manager of the Pet Palace, didn't give her an opportunity to answer. "You didn't think he" — he threw a scornful glance at Martin — "could carry this off on his own, did you?" He laughed harshly. "You fool," Jerry said, directing the words to Martin. "You led her right here. And you" — he turned to Carla — "you just couldn't stay out of it, could you? Too bad you've got no one to blame but yourself. I warned you. Twice."

She jerked back as he waved a gun at her. "You pushed me in front of the truck."

"Not me. I hired someone to do it."

"Why, Jerry?" She gestured around her.

"For a smart lady, you sure ask stupid

questions. Money, Reverend. You know about money, don't you? The filthy lucre that all you Bible-spouting types warn against."

Martin took a step forward. "Let her go, Jerry. It's over."

Jerry leveled the gun at him. "You're right. It's over. For you." He fired.

Martin slumped to the floor. Quietly. So quietly that it was almost surreal. Surely when one person took the life of another, there should some kind of noise. Some kind of something.

Carla started toward him, but Jerry trained the gun on her. "Forget him."

She ignored him and bent over Martin. She found a pulse, faint but there all the same. "He's still alive."

"He won't be fore long." Jerry jerked her up, wrenching her arm.

She cried out, but he continued to twist her arm until she ceased struggling. "You can't just leave him."

"Why not?"

She looked at Jerry in horror. "He could bleed to death." She cast one more glance at Martin, at the paleness of his face, and corrected herself. "*Is* bleeding to death."

"And I'm supposed to care?"

She carefully ignored that. "Please — just

let me call someone."

"Think again, lady. You're not calling any-one."

A whimper from one of the cages caught her attention. "What about the dogs?"

"What about them?"

"You have to let them go."

He gave her a taunting grin. "I don't have to do nothing."

"They'll starve."

"They won't starve. They're going to make a contribution to science. A once in a lifetime contribution, if you get my drift."

Carla looked at this man whom she'd known for years. How had she not noticed the coldness of his eyes before now? They were as lifeless as the concrete floor, now stained with Martin's blood.

She wouldn't beg for herself. But she had more than her own life to consider now. Her gaze strayed to Martin's still form and then to the dogs. "Please — don't do this."

"It won't work."

"What?"

"That big-eyed look you use to get what you want. You care so much about him, maybe you'd like to die with him. Now."

She strained against him, but he only gripped her arm harder.

"Your choice."

"You're sick, Jerry."

"No. I'm free. At last."

He nudged her with the gun. She darted one last look at Martin. Had she seen his arm twitch? It must have been her imagination, for he was completely motionless now.

"Please — just let me see to Martin before we go."

"What are you going to do? Pray him back to life? You're not that good, preacher." He grinned insolently. "I've heard your Sunday sermons."

Jerry shouldered open the door, keeping the gun trained on her. He was so close to her that she felt his breath whispering across her cheek. It was hot and smelled of beer and onions. Fear and revulsion swelled in her throat, nearly causing her to gag.

"Get it together," he ordered roughly.

Outside, she inhaled deeply, the fresh air ridding her of the nausea.

A white van with the Pet Palace logo painted on it was parked outside. If she allowed him to force her inside, she had very little chance of getting away. She looked around. Where would she run to? Jerry had already proved he was capable of anything. Still, she stood a better chance outside than locked inside the van with him.

"You got any ideas about running, you

can forget them," he said, apparently guessing her thoughts. "There's no place to run." He pushed her inside and slid in beside her.

She had no choice but to scoot across the seat. As he switched the gun to the other hand, she edged away from him. If she could get the passenger door open, she might . . .

He snaked out an arm to grab her wrist. "No, you don't. You're not going anywhere." He gave her a twisted smile as he yanked her against him, causing her to shudder at his nearness. "Leastways, not alone. You and me are taking a nice little ride. Together."

He drove at a moderate pace, destroying her hope that he might speed and attract the attention of a police car.

She slid a glance his way. If she could get him to talk, she might distract him enough that he'd make a mistake. His cocky grin spoke volumes about his arrogance. It shouldn't be too hard to play on his vanity.

She schooled her voice to one of admiration. "How did you get the idea of selling pets to research labs?"

He looked pleased at the question. "I read a lot. Not much else to do in that stinking store besides taking care of the animals and answering stupid questions. I read that labs are hurting for subjects. I just decided to supply them."

"You're really clever."

"Yeah. Too bad my old man didn't realize that."

"How long have you been in the . . . supply business?"

"Going on three years now. I got enough money saved up to start over somewhere else. Good thing too, since you stuck your nose in."

She wasn't a good enough actress to hide her disgust. "I understand why Martin did what he did, but you . . ." She looked at him in contempt. "All you care about is the money."

"You're real smart, know that, preacher?"

She ignored his sarcasm. "Selling people's pets to labs for money. How do you live with yourself?"

"Easy. I just think of all those whining people and their yapping pets over the years. They owe me. They owe me big."

"No one stole from you, no one did anything to hurt you. We were your friends."

"That's right. No one did anything except to yell at me if something wasn't in that they needed. Good old Jerry. Always there to open up the store when someone needed a new goldfish to replace the one that died because their kid decided to put bubble bath in the tank. You know what, preacher? I got tired."

"Tired?"

"Yeah. Tired of treating sick animals because the owners were too cheap to take them to the vet. Tired of cleaning up after stinking animals. Tired of catering to rich old women who had nothing better to do than buy fancy collars for their dogs."

"Why didn't you get out? Do something else?" She kept her gaze focused straight ahead. She didn't dare look at Jerry's face. Even a glimpse of the coldness in his eyes would undermine her nerve. And right now she needed every bit of courage she possessed.

"I don't *know* anything else, lady. I've worked in that pet store since I was fifteen. Fifteen. More than half my life, and what have I got to show for it? Nothing. A big fat nothing. Well, no more. Once I deliver these mutts, I'll be sitting pretty.

"You know the beauty of it? I can do it anywhere. When things get too hot here, I move on. Set up business somewhere else."

The van slowed as he negotiated a sharp turn. It was now or never. Carla lifted the latch to the door and pushed it open, flinging herself out of the van. Remembering what she'd learned as a child in gymnastic classes, she bent her knees and kept her chin tucked under as she rolled away from the van.

As soon as she was clear of the car, she pushed herself up and started to run. Her wet clothes hampered her movement, dragging her down. Her feet slid on the soggy ground. She heard the van not far behind her.

Jerry opened the door, catching Carla across the middle with it and knocking her down. She lay there in the mud, winded and aching, unable to move even when she heard him tromp over the ground toward her. He jerked her to her feet.

"Had to make it harder on yourself, didn't you?" He clamped an arm around her neck. "Move."

Automatically she resisted, digging her heels in the ground. The cool hardness of the piece of metal pressed in her side caused her to slip.

He tightened his hold, propelling her forward. "I said move."

She regained her footing but pretended to stumble.

"If you prefer, we can end it here. It's your call."

Knowing she had no choice, she walked back to the car. Her heels sank into the soft ground, and she fell to her knees. This time her fall was not contrived, and she winced as she hit the ground.

He yanked her up.

She felt her leg give way. "I think I've sprained my ankle."

The gun pressed closer.

"It's not a trick."

"Too bad." He forced her into the van and shoved her onto the passenger seat. "Another stunt like that and I'll shoot you."

Her ankle throbbing, Carla sank back into the seat and tried to think. Sam would find her. He'd discover she was missing. He'd try the usual places first, and when he found she wasn't at any of those . . .

She shook her head, forcing herself to face reality. Sam had no idea where she was. How could he? She'd taken off on her own, with scarcely a thought to the consequences. And she had no one to blame but herself. Herself and her own stubborn insistence that she could handle anything. A soft laugh that was half a sob escaped her lips. So far all she'd managed to handle was getting Martin shot and herself taken hostage by a man who'd made it clear he wouldn't hesitate to kill her.

"Where are you taking me?" she asked.

"You'll see."

She was afraid she did.

Sam shifted in Emma's seat and tried for at least the hundredth time to get comfortable. The twinge in his leg that had started awhile ago had developed into a full-fledged charley horse. He reached down to rub his calf and banged his head against the steering wheel. He attempted to stretch his leg, only to knock it on the console. Again.

He muttered something under his breath and gave in to the temptation of fantasizing about replacing Emma with a real car. He shook his head, dismissing the idea immediately. Carla loved this car. After all, she'd named it after her grandmother.

He rotated his shoulders and immediately regretted it. It only served to remind him of the kink in his neck. Detective work wasn't what it was cracked up to be. Watching the house had netted him a permanent backache, a leg that had more knots in it than a sailor's rope, and a caffeine hangover. He was punchy with fatigue and worry.

And no Martin.

The curtains parted. Sam slouched down in the car as far as possible. He peered over the dashboard at the thud of a door being closed. Thelma Harvey, pink curlers in her hair and an apron tied around her middle, advanced on him.

"Uh oh."

She knocked on the window. Reluctantly he rolled it down.

"Sam Hastings. What are you doing out here spying on me?"

He grimaced as he pulled himself up, promptly banging his head on the roof of the car.

"I wasn't exactly spying —"

"What exactly were you doing?"

"Do you know where Martin is?"

"Martin? What's Martin got to do with this?"

"Is he inside?"

Thelma's gaze strayed to the house. "No."

"Do you know where he is?"

She planted her hands on her hips. "I'm not saying another word until you tell me what's going on."

"Carla's missing."

Thelma didn't look particularly upset. "I wouldn't worry. She's probably out visiting someone."

He held on to his temper. Carla was missing because she'd tried to help this woman find her dog. Then he noticed the distress in Thelma's eyes. "What's wrong?"

"Martin and I had a fight. He goes out

and doesn't say where. And there are the calls."

"What kind of calls?"

"The kind he can't tell me about."

"Do you have any idea where he is now?"

"If I knew where he was, I wouldn't be standing here discussing it with you, now would I?" The asperity was back in her voice, only to vanish when she asked, "You think Martin's got something to do with Carla's absence?"

"I don't know," Sam said as honestly as possible.

She gripped his arm. "Where's my grandson?"

He gently eased himself from her grasp. "I don't know," he said again.

"You think he's involved in something — something bad, don't you?"

He looked at the fierce glare in her eyes. She didn't deserve a lie. But was the truth any better?

"Don't you?" she persisted when he remained silent.

"Yes, I do."

"Thank you," she said at last.

"For what?"

"For not lying to an old lady." She sighed, a sound so packed with sadness that it tore at his heart. "Come on in."

"I can't —"

"I found something in Martin's room. When he left this morning, I got worried. I started looking around . . ."

Sam was out of the car before she finished.

He spared a moment to glance around Martin's room. It was Spartan, almost barren, with none of the usual paraphernalia associated with a young man still in school.

"Here it is." Thelma handed him a thin folder.

He flipped through it. The list of dates was there. All it did was confirm what he already knew. He needed more. Something like an address.

"Is this what you're looking for?" Thelma asked, handing him a hastily drawn map scrawled in a notebook.

"I hope so," he said fervently. He bent to brush his lips against the paper-thin skin of her cheek. "Thank you."

She seemed to sag before his eyes, her once bright eyes now bleary and unfocused. "Bring him home to me. Please."

"I'll try."

Sunlight poked its way through the clouds, reflecting off the rain-slick streets with blinding intensity. Sam shaded his eyes with his hand, keeping the other on the steering wheel while he scanned the road for the turnoff. When he saw it, he swerved the wheel sharply.

The road, hardly more than a rutted path, twisted back and forth. It took all his skill to keep the little car on the dirt lane and out of the brush bordering it. The grade steepened, and he shifted into third. He gripped the steering wheel, his knuckles whitening under the pressure, then he saw it.

The building barely warranted a second look, with its corrugated tin roof, rusted siding, and dirty windows. It was so nondescript, it almost blended into the passing countryside. Almost missing the turn, Sam yanked on the steering wheel. He winced as the wheels squealed. So much for approaching quietly.

Abandoning stealth for speed, he slammed the door, ran to the building, and tested the door. To his surprise, it opened easily. He smelled the dogs first and then heard them. Before he could check on them, he saw a man lying on the floor. Even from here, Sam could see the bloodstain on his shirt. Martin.

He felt for a pulse and found a faint one. He pulled a handkerchief from his pocket and pressed it against the wound, staunching the flow of blood. He yanked off his jacket and laid it under the other man's head.

"Martin, can you hear me?"

Martin's eyelids fluttered open. "Sam?"

"Where's Carla?"

"Jerry . . ."

"Jerry? Jerry Foster? Did he do this?"

Martin managed a nod. "Took her." He grabbed Sam's hand. "Must believe . . . didn't mean for it to . . ."

"I believe you."

Martin's eyes drifted shut.

Sam shook him gently. "Do you have any idea where Jerry could have taken her?"

"Store. Has to go back there. For . . . money."

He leaned closer to catch the words. "The Pet Palace?"

Again, Martin nodded. "Find her."

Sam pressed Martin's hand. "I will. I'll get an ambulance. Can you hang on until it gets here?"

"Yeah." The last word came as a gasp.

Still, Sam hesitated.

Martin grabbed at Sam's shirt, pulling himself up. "G-go. Now."

Sam eased Martin down. He didn't have a choice. If he didn't get to Carla before Jerry decided he didn't need her anymore

. . . He refused to finish the thought. He'd find her. He had to.

The car bumped over the road as he pressed harder on the accelerator. He knew he was pushing it — going this fast over the deeply grooved lane. He chanced ripping the suspension out of the car.

Swerving onto the main road, he started putting it together. It wasn't hard to guess Jerry's reason for stealing the dogs. Research labs paid big money for subjects. Sam slammed his hand against the dashboard. Why hadn't he figured it out before now? Jerry was in a perfect position to know who owned pets.

Sam slammed on the brakes as a deer bounded across the highway. He barely avoided hitting the animal. Carla would be pleased, he thought, that he hadn't run into the deer. She treasured all life. His hands tightened on the steering wheel as he thought about how Jerry had left Martin to bleed to death. He dared not think what Jerry had planned for Carla.

Martin's part in the scheme was more complex. At a guess, Sam would say he had done it out of some misguided idea to help medical research.

As he approached the freeway, he saw a small gas station with a pay phone out front.

He spared a few precious minutes to dial the emergency number and give Martin's location.

He was halfway back to Saratoga when he realized he was praying aloud. Another change Carla had brought into his life. At one time he would have been embarrassed to discover he was praying with all the fervency of a child. Now he accepted it, welcomed it. Praying was all he could do for her right now.

He didn't try to make sense of the words. He repeated them until they ran together in a litany of pleading, grasping them as he would a live preserver. If he stopped, he doubted he'd be able to hold on to his sanity.

As he approached Saratoga's city limits, he focused his thoughts. He couldn't afford to be distracted, not when Carla's life depended on what he did in the next few minutes.

The Pet Palace looked strange with its drawn shades and lack of midday activity. After parking the car a block away, he made his way back to the store by way of a back alley.

Peering through a window, he looked inside.

Nothing.

He tried the door, jiggling the lock. It gave way.

"Come in, Councilman. We've been expecting you."

CHAPTER TEN

The scene was out of a bad nightmare. Jerry had an arm clamped around Carla's neck, a gun pressed to her temple.

Sam forced himself to breathe and to think beyond the panic that threatened to paralyze him. Giving way to his fear wouldn't help Carla. He searched her face for signs of fear. The brave smile she gave him twisted his heart. Even now, she was more concerned for him than she was for herself. Later, when she was safe, he'd give her a lecture about going off on her own. He only hoped there would be a later.

"Looks like an old-fashioned standoff," Jerry said.

"Drop it, Jerry."

Jerry laughed, a harsh sound that grated against Carla's nerves. "You got it backward. I'm holding all the cards." He drew his arm tighter around her neck, emphasizing his point.

For a moment she feared she would pass out, but she managed to hold on. She lifted her head and met Sam's gaze. Her fear gave way to anger. The anguish on his face only served to fuel it. She wasn't going to let herself be used against him. If only she had a weapon . . .

She looked down. The heels of her shoes. Those wretched heels that had caused her to wrench her ankle. She ground her heel into Jerry's instep. With a howl of pain, he staggered, his grip slackening enough for her to push away from him, jabbing him in the ribs with her elbow as she did so. His yowl of pain gave her a rush of satisfaction.

Before she could register it fully, she felt herself being jerked out of the way. She spun around in time to see Sam slam his fist into Jerry's face and follow it up with a blow to the gut. Blood trickling from his mouth, Jerry crumpled to the ground, the gun skittering across the floor. Sam had yanked him up and started to hit him again when a soft pressure on his arm made him pause.

"He's not worth it."

He looked at Carla and saw the pleading in her eyes. "You're right."

Sam spared one last glance at Jerry, who was now whimpering in pain. He then looked down at his hands, which were shaking with anger and fear. He never wanted to feel this kind of rage again. It tainted his mouth with a bitter taste. Deliberately he backed up a step, putting distance between himself and Jerry.

"I'm all right," he said and found it was true.

Her sigh of relief told him just how worried she'd been.

He found some packaging tape and bound Jerry's hands and feet. When he was certain that Jerry was securely bound, Sam pulled Carla into his arms and crushed her to him. He couldn't help himself. Not trusting his eyes, he ran his hands over her, searching for injuries.

"You're all right?" His voice trembled on the words.

"I am now."

His expression changed from concern to anger. "You ever go off like that again —" His anger died as soon as it flared to life. Carla was safe. Nothing else mattered.

"We've got to help Martin. Jerry shot him, but he might still be alive."

Sam struggled to find enough charity in him to forgive the man who'd put her life in jeopardy. Martin had a lot to answer for. "I already found him. He's going to be all right."

She must have understood what he was feeling, for she laid her hand on his arm. "He was doing what he felt was right, Sam. He's not like Jerry."

"Yeah." Someday, *maybe,* he'd be able to accept that. For now, it was enough that Carla was here with him. He shuddered, remembering just how close he'd come to losing her. He pulled her to him and kissed her. "Let's call the police. Tell them we've got some garbage for them to pick up."

She turned within a few minutes. "They're on their way."

Jerry squirmed against his bonds and managed to push himself up to a half sitting position. "I had a sweet thing going until you two stuck your noses into it. You think you're so smart." His laugh came out more like a grunt of pain. "All you've got on me is taking a few dogs."

"Try kidnapping and attempted murder," Sam said, considering punching Jerry in the face again. He could almost taste the satisfaction of planting his fist on the other man's mouth.

Jerry's bravado faded as he slumped back to the floor.

Sam turned to Carla. A look at her face

caused him to draw in a sharp breath. She looked more fragile than ever, her eyes huge and dark against her pale skin. All he wanted to do was take her home and pamper her, but they couldn't leave until the police showed up.

He looked up as a siren sounded in the distance. He jerked Jerry to his feet. When the police arrived, Sam briefly explained the situation. A sergeant read Jerry his rights and handcuffed him. He spat obscenities at Carla, nearly causing Sam to change his mind about beating Jerry senseless. A relieved sigh shuddered from Carla as an officer hauled Jerry away in a patrol car.

The sergeant took their statements, cautioned them to make themselves available for additional questioning, then let them go.

"We need to tell Thelma," Carla said.

Sam nodded, his plans to take her home and put her to bed dissolving. He knew she'd never leave Thelma to face this alone.

An hour later, she was repeating the story to Thelma. The older woman had aged ten years in the last few minutes.

Carla gripped Thelma's hand and pressed it. "Martin's going to be all right —"

"How could he do something like this? He was such a good boy, always calling me, checking up on me. How could he take

Grover Cleveland and all those other dogs?"

Tears trickled down her cheek. For the first time since Carla had known the old lady, Thelma didn't wipe them away with her perennial linen handkerchief. She seemed totally unaware of them.

"None of this changes what he feels for you," Sam said gently.

Thelma looked at him gratefully. "I have to go to him . . . see him."

"We'll take you," Carla said.

Thelma leaned heavily on them as they escorted her to the car.

The scene at the hospital was a bittersweet one. After reassuring herself that Martin would be all right, Thelma broke down again. Carla stayed with her through the evening, until Mrs. Miller took her place.

"You go on home now," Mrs. Miller said. "I'll stay with Thelma."

Carla accepted gratefully. She'd tried to send Sam home hours ago, but he'd refused. Now was the time for reckoning.

The ride home was quiet. Too quiet, she thought uneasily. Sam had every right to be furious with her. She'd broken her promise, nearly getting both of them killed in the process.

"Let's get it over with," she said. "Go ahead and yell me."

"The only thing I want to do is this." He kissed her. And kissed her again.

She held on to him. "Love me?"

"Always."

Returning the pets to their owners made everything worthwhile, Carla decided, smiling as Mrs. Miller fussed over Collette. The same scene was repeated with Thelma and Grover Cleveland.

"You'll never know . . ." The older woman choked over the words. "Thank you for putting in a good word for Martin." She turned to Sam. "And you, Sam, for getting him a lawyer. I didn't know what we were going to do, but . . ." She dabbed at her eyes with her handkerchief.

Carla hugged her. "Martin's going to be all right. And so is Grover Cleveland."

The dog licked the old lady's face.

Thelma cuddled him to her. "Come here, precious."

Later, Carla blinked away tears as she watched the Sandbergs fuss over Samson.

"Thank you." Ethan's voice stumbled over the words as he reached for Maude's hand.

Carla felt her own heart stumble at the joy in the older couple's eyes. She looked at Sam and saw the same response mirrored in his eyes. She held out her hand. When he squeezed it, her heart swelled.

Sam watched Carla fidget. It wasn't like her. She had something to tell him. He was sure of it. He'd given her every opportunity, yet she still hesitated.

At last he slipped his arms around her waist, bringing her to him. "What's so terrible you can't tell me?"

"It's not terrible," she whispered. "It's so wonderful that I can't find the words." She took his hands and pressed them to her stomach.

The significance of the act didn't register until he looked at her eyes. They were brimming with tears. Tears and happiness. He hardly dared hope. . . .

"Does this mean what I think it does?" he asked, his voice so husky that it was more of a croak.

She nodded. "Are you happy?"

"Happy doesn't begin to cover it." He caught her by the waist and swung her around. Abruptly realizing what he'd done, he set her down. "Did I hurt you?"

Her soft laugh wrapped its way around his heart. "I'm pregnant, Sam. Not sick."

He swept her up into his arms.

"Where are we going?"

"I'm taking you to bed. You need to rest."

She laid her head on his shoulder. "You're crazy, you know that?"

"I'm entitled. I'm about to become a father."

"Not for another eight months."

With infinite gentleness, he laid her on the bed. He knelt by the bed and framed her face with his palms. "Have I mentioned that I love you?"

"Maybe a time or two."

"Definitely not enough." He kissed her, long and deep. "I love you."

"Me too."

EPILOGUE

"We have here a fine specimen of early eighteenth-century workmanship," the auctioneer announced. "Who will start the bidding at five hundred dollars?"

A numbered card was raised.

Carla listened in amazement as the bidding quickly escalated to twenty-five hundred dollars. By the end of the auction, they'd raised thirty thousand dollars.

Too excited to wait, she found Jeanette. "You did it."

"*We* did it," her mother-in-law corrected. "And this is just the beginning. I've got an idea for a bachelor auction. We'll get all the eligible bachelors in the city. . . ." Her voice trailed off as she looked uncertainly at Carla. "That is, if it's all right with you?"

Carla hugged her mother-in-law. "You're wonderful. Come on. Let's find Sam and go celebrate."

Jeanette smiled. "You go ahead. I have a

feeling you two have some celebrating of your own to do."

"Is it that obvious?"

Sam's mother kissed Carla's cheek. "Be happy, and let me know when I can start bragging about becoming a grandmother."

Sam watched the easy camaraderie between his mother and Carla. A warmth settled around his heart as he remembered the news Carla had given him that morning. He had it all — blessings more than he could count.

She headed to him and tucked her arm in his. "We did it."

"When was the last time I told you how much I love you?"

She screwed up her face in thought. "Not since this morning."

"We'll have to correct that." He kissed her. "You're beautiful. I love you." He placed his hand over her still-flat stomach. Someday he'd feel the life that even now grew there.

He caught her hand. "Come on. We're going home, Mrs. Hastings."

Home.

Her fingers tightened around his. "I thought you'd never ask."

ABOUT THE AUTHOR

Jane McBride Choate has been weaving stories in her head ever since she can remember, but she shelved her dreams of writing to marry and start a family. After her third child was born, she wrote a short story and submitted it to a children's magazine. To her astonishment, it was accepted. Two children later, she is still creating stories. She believes in the healing power of love, which is why she writes romances. Jane and her husband, Larry, live with their five children in Loveland, Colorado.

The employees of Thorndike Press hope you have enjoyed this Large Print book. All our Thorndike and Wheeler Large Print titles are designed for easy reading, and all our books are made to last. Other Thorndike Press Large Print books are available at your library, through selected bookstores, or directly from us.

For information about titles, please call:

(800) 223-1244

or visit our Web site at:

www.gale.com/thorndike
www.gale.com/wheeler

To share your comments, please write:

Publisher
Thorndike Press
295 Kennedy Memorial Drive
Waterville, ME 04901